The idea of humbling Danton was intoxicating

"The truth is...I don't live in fear of anything, Danton," Bernadette said in a bored tone. "I simply find you insufferable."

The insult amused him. "You told me that once before. And I didn't believe you then. We danced too well together, Bernadette."

The memory burned through her mind. He had held her so close, made her so terribly aware of his body, and her own. But she'd been much younger then...inexperienced.

"I'm not as interested in frivolous activities as you are," she said scornfully.

"Indeed." His eyes twinkled wickedly. "Then let me offer you a contest in character. I will unmask you...see your true identity...before you can detect mine." His smile was teasingly confident. "We shall see who is right...and wrong."

EMMA DARCY nearly became an actress until her fiancé declared he preferred to attend the theater *with* her. She became a wife and mother. Later she took up oil painting—unsuccessfully, she remarks. Then, she tried architecture, designing the family home in New South Wales. Next came romance writing—"the hardest and most challenging of all the activities," she confesses.

Books by Emma Darcy

HARLEQUIN PRESENTS

984—DON'T ASK ME NOW
999—THE UNPREDICTABLE MAN
1020—THE WRONG MIRROR
1033—THE ONE THAT GOT AWAY
1048—STRIKE AT THE HEART
1080—THE POSITIVE APPROACH
1103—MISTRESS OF PILLATORO
1151—ALWAYS LOVE
1177—A PRICELESS LOVE
1199—THE ALOHA BRIDE
1232—THE FALCON'S MISTRESS

HARLEQUIN ROMANCE

2900—BLIND DATE
2941—WHIRLPOOL OF PASSION

EMMA DARCY

the power and the passion

Harlequin Books

TORONTO • NEW YORK • LONDON
AMSTERDAM • PARIS • SYDNEY • HAMBURG
STOCKHOLM • ATHENS • TOKYO • MILAN

This book is dedicated
to all those fine people
who shared a magical night
with us in Boston.
But most especially to Jennifer
who was kind enough to share with us
one of her dreams.

Harlequin Presents first edition June 1990
ISBN 0-373-11272-6

Original hardcover edition published in 1989
by Mills & Boon Limited

CHAPTER ONE

NOT again!

Bernadette's teeth clenched in sheer frustration as she stared at the sheaf of red roses in the delivery boy's arms. She knew, without having to count them, that there would be twenty-four this time.

'Miss Bernadette Hamilton?'

'Yes,' she bit out, unable to respond to the fatuous grin on the boy's face.

She inwardly winced over the curtness of her acknowledgement as his grin disappeared. The boy was only doing a job. He wasn't to know that the beautiful blooms gave her more torment than pleasure. She offered an appeasing smile as he gravely handed her the roses and the gold-embossed envelope—sealed, as it had been every year, with wax.

Bernadette didn't bother to ask who was the donor. She had pursued that track three years ago and the florist knew no more about the mystery man than she did. The envelope was sent with a typed note of instructions and a bank cheque—untraceable.

She dragged her gaze up from the wax seal and caught the sparkle of suppressed laughter in the delivery boy's eyes. 'Thank you,' she said with almost frigid dignity, instantly realising that the curious once-a-year incident was probably a source of amusing gossip at the florist shop.

Being Gerard Hamilton's illegitimate daughter carried enough notoriety. Her stupid and indiscreet attempt to identify the sender had almost certainly turned a routine transaction into a memorable one.

The delivery boy gave her a whimsical—or was it a mocking?—half-bow, and retreated towards the lifts. Bernadette grimaced at his swaggering back. Only after he had gone did she step back into her apartment and slam the door shut, giving vent to some of her bitter frustration.

This was the sixth time. She almost hated the man who was doing it to her, whoever he was. The roses she could have dismissed. Anyone could be sending her roses on her birthday—one for each year of her age since she had turned nineteen—if only the gold-embossed envelope did not come with them.

What he was doing to her—what he had done to her —with his tantalising messages was diabolical. They had completely undermined her relationships with Scott and Barry and Trent; made her wonder about every other man who had apparently been attracted to her . . . whether it was for her own self, or because of their potential prospects as Gerard Hamilton's future son-in-law. Even if she was illegitimate, it seemed that any foot inside her father's door would do.

Bernadette had suffered too many lessons in disillusion to accept much at face value any more. But this insidious siege on her heart and mind . . . why didn't he make himself known to her? Why taunt her with words of love if he had no intention of meeting her . . . openly declaring what he secretly and mysteriously professed?

It was madness! Mean . . . eccentric . . . selfish . . . and positively infuriating. Perhaps he was psychotic!

The thought had crossed Bernadette's mind before. She pondered it again as she filled a vase with water and jammed the roses into it; roses so darkly red they were almost purple, and so deeply scented they were an invasion of her privacy, the aroma quickly stealing to every recess of the spacious apartment.

Not psychotic, she decided. At the hospital where she had been working she had dealt with people who were mentally unbalanced. The game this man was playing was too patterned, too deliberately paced to have been conceived by a sick mind. This was someone diabolically clever . . . ruthlessly determined to infiltrate and influence her life . . . and acting out of purposeful self-interest.

Undoubtedly a fortune-hunter.

Possibly trying to climb on to some non-existent bandwagon. When he did declare himself, as he obviously must, she would know how to deal with him!

Bernadette swept up the vase of roses and dumped it on to the centre of the white stone coffee-table in the living-room. They looked sumptuous . . . wrong . . . out of place with the light modern décor.

Her eyes skated over the white leather sofas and floppy cushions—the choice of the interior decorator who had been hired by her father to furnish the apartment. Cold and clinical and emotionless, Bernadette thought. Just like her father.

She had always hated living here, hated the necessity of accepting this apartment from him until she finished her studies and could earn her own living. But it had been worth it to get her medical degree. That could never be taken away from her, and she would put it to good use. Better than any other use her father had for his money!

However, it was a matter of pride that when she handed this apartment back to her father—as she would do within a month or two—it would not have been changed in any way. He would get it back precisely as he had given it to her!

And wherever she went she would make herself a real home, a place that was cosy and welcoming, where roses could look right and . . .

Bernadette's fantasy came to a jolting halt. He was doing it to her again! She was letting his damned roses infiltrate her mind, making her think of things she had never had, stirring needs . . .

She picked up the envelope, stared down at it, her fingers sliding indecisively over the wax seal. Better for her peace of mind if she refused to read what he had written. She should toss the envelope away, burn it, deny him the insidious fascination he worked on her. It was the sensible thing to do.

But Bernadette had never backed away from a challenge in her life, even to the extent of defying her father . . . and she was fairly certain that no one else in the world had got away with that. She had been only twelve years old at the time and it had been her first meeting with him. Twelve lonely years of having her existence completely ignored, and then . . .

Her mouth thinned in determination. Her fierce independence had been hard won, and she would stand up to any man . . . or woman, if necessary. She was not going to let anyone intimidate her, particularly not a man who needed to keep to the shadows of anonymity.

Irritation with his impertinence made her rip open the flap of the envelope with total disregard for the expensiveness of the paper. She withdrew its contents with an angry sense of impatience . . . exactly the same style of card as on previous years . . . a shimmering gold . . . luminous red print in the beautifully flowing strokes of copperplate handwriting.

Happy birthday
Bernadette—
my love.

As she opened the card Bernadette instinctively braced herself against the impact of this year's message. His words had a way of worming into her subconsciousness and tripping through her mind at unexpected moments; unsettling her judgements and slanting her perspective with a most unwelcome persistence. It was another invasion, of a kind she found impossible to fight. And that was the core of her frustration!

Her eyes skimmed over the unusually short verse, then backtracked to read the words again and again.

> The power and the passion of life
> is in loving.
> Embrace the power;
> Savour the passion.
> All else . . . is vanity!

A sense of outrage grew as Bernadette furiously dissected their meaning. Was he suggesting that it was only a vanity to have spent all these years of hard work earning her medical degree? That she should have spent that time loving him instead? And precisely where would that have got her? Bernadette thought scornfully—out on a limb, depending on him not to drop her when he felt like it!

From the time in her life when she could first comprehend what was going on about her, she was determined to stand on her own two feet and not depend on anyone. For anything! And she had done it!

A flash of anger burned through her. It wasn't her fault that love was in short supply where she was concerned. She hadn't asked to be born on the wrong side of the blanket to a man like Gerard Hamilton. She hadn't wanted her mother to die before she was old enough to remember her. And as for passion, it was all too easily generated when there was wealth in the background; and other people savouring that had proved a bitter exercise for her.

If she had ever counted on loving to be the power and passion of her life, she would be in a very sorry state. And if that was what her anonymous lover really thought, she would soon disabuse him once she had the opportunity.

She tossed the card into the drawer where she kept the others and determined not to look at any of them ever again. Not even when she felt lonely or sad, nor when she suffered the occasional bouts of deep depression.

One day he would reveal himself, and she would confront him with them. She knew all the words by heart and she would certainly put his sincerity to the test. She would demand to know why he had sent them, and what he meant by them, and she would get the truth out of him if it was the last thing she did!

The doorbell rang again.

Bernadette's heart gave an agitated leap and she took a deep breath to restore a façade of calm composure.

It would certainly be her father this time.

She strode quickly into her bedroom for a last-minute check on her appearance. Not that she should care what he thought of her. She had learnt to do without his caring since infancy. But some wisp of pride demanded that she not look inferior to his legitimate daughter whenever her father escorted her out in public. Alicia Hamilton was the darling of the social pages. Bernadette never would be. She scorned such empty nonsense, yet she had it thrust upon her. There was no getting away from the Press when her father was so newsworthy . . . Gerard Hamilton, with a finger in every corporate pie, a financial network that spread across the world, and always making profits, of course; more money to become bigger and richer and more powerful.

Had he bought her mother, in the same way as he had bought all his other mistresses since his wife had died? Bernadette fiercely wanted to know, but she never asked . . . never would ask . . . not anything of him. Not ever!

The blue ice of her eyes hardened at the thought. Her reflection in the hall mirror assured her that not a wisp of her dark blonde hair had escaped from the elegant coil, that her make-up was as perfect as it could be, and the white dinner-gown draped itself over the lissom curves of her body with all the style and grace of its elegant line.

Yes, she was ready for her father . . . ready for anybody, ready to meet any of them on any ground . . . and hold her own.

She walked unhurriedly from her bedroom, picked up her handbag from the hall table, and opened the door.

CHAPTER TWO

GERARD HAMILTON was a big man: tall, broad-shouldered, barrel-chested, as overwhelming in his size as in the strength of his personality. He was a hard man to oppose; a powerful man, used to winning his own way; a man whose fifty-eight years of age sat easily on him, a testament of experience and assured maturity that even enhanced the rugged male attraction that had always been his.

No wonder women ran after him, adored him, would do anything for him. Bernadette could see his drawing power, even feel it sometimes, but she was never going to let herself be vulnerable to it.

Gerard Hamilton smiled at the tall, proud carriage of his daughter, approved the stubborn tilt of her chin, admired the undaunted challenge in her wide steady eyes, the disciplined sweep of her hairstyle, the striking purity of features that gave her face such a cool, remote beauty . . . so like Odile, even to the soft womanliness of her figure.

But her mind was his . . . that sharp intellect that stood back and weighed, and could act with ruthless ferocity if it wanted to . . . or needed to. His child . . . as the others weren't and never would be, although he didn't doubt he had fathered them. They were as useless and shallow and petty as his wife had been. But this one . . . she was his.

And he knew that in the dark recesses of her mind there was a hatred for him, because of what she thought he had done. Too late to correct that impression now. There was no proof. No way he could prove to her satisfaction what had really happened.

Besides, he had put together far too many deals in his time to know that it might not be such a bad thing. Life often tricked you . . . when you got the things you thought you wanted and they didn't turn out to be what you wanted anyway. Like his legitimate children.

He swept the thought away and set himself to enjoy this evening's duel with Bernadette.

'You look more lovely with every year that passes,' he said with sincere appreciation. 'Happy birthday, my dear.'

'Thank you, Father,' Bernadette replied coolly.

He didn't attempt to kiss her cheek. Her reserve was impregnable and he knew that any gesture of affection from him would only be suffered with contempt. He admired her independence but sometimes he regretted it, too deeply to allow much contemplation. Easier not to think about it.

He held out the car-keys. 'A present for you.'

Bernadette took them, weighing them in her hand, wanting to thrust them back at him but knowing there was a better way to show her disdain for the way he used his wealth.

He smiled. It was the confident smile of a man who knew he could buy anything he fancied. 'It's a red Mercedes sports. You can drive me to dinner.'

'Thank you. But you do know I'll sell it?' Bernadette said bluntly.

As she had every other car he had bought her, and given the money to needy causes. Her mind instantly flitted to the women's shelter where she was called all too frequently to attend to women and children who required medical help. Yes, the shelter could certainly do with an injection of capital.

'The car is yours, Bernadette. What you do with it is entirely your business,' Gerard said without the slightest umbrage.

Which showed precisely how little it meant to him! Cars . . . furs . . . jewellery . . . just standard barter in the game of getting his own way. Had her mother succumbed to Gerard Hamilton because of what he could give her? Had there been any love involved at all? There couldn't have been from him. Only a man who had no love in him could have turned his back on his own child for twelve years, as he had done.

She wondered why he had bothered with her these last twelve years. He had certainly not been motivated by a sudden rush of love. No doubt he had some plan for her future. Gerard Hamilton didn't make investments if he didn't expect some profit or other. But he would never win her over with his expensive gifts. Not in a million years!

She looked him straight in the eye and told him precisely what she thought. 'I wish you wouldn't do it, Father. You'll never buy me.'

He gave a soft laugh. 'Don't ever change, Bernadette. If you did . . .' His mouth took on an ironic twist. 'Then I'd have nothing at all.'

Bernadette frowned over the remark as she pulled the apartment door shut behind her. 'Nothing?' she tossed back at him as they began to walk towards the lifts. 'I thought you liked the power your wealth gives you. That's something surely.'

'Yes. But wealth and power are a vanity, Bernadette. I like to be on top. Always have. But the passion for it . . .' he paused, then softly, almost to himself '. . . left me a long time ago. Twenty-four years ago, in fact.'

The doors in front of them opened and Bernadette stepped inside the lift, hiding her shock as best she could. Power . . . passion . . . vanity . . . they were the key words from the verse! Was it her father who had been sending the roses and those cards all this time? But why? What possible motive could he have?

Loving . . . he hadn't mentioned that! Was love what he wanted from her? Twenty-four roses . . . twenty-four years ago . . . but he hadn't taken any notice of her until she was twelve years old. He had certainly paid for her to be looked after, saw that she wanted for nothing . . . but loving had never come into it!

The lift opened on to the basement car park and Bernadette blindly accompanied her father to the red Mercedes sports car. He opened the door on the driver's side. Bernadette slid in behind the wheel, her heart palpitating so fast that she had difficulty breathing. She tried to calm down, but it was too late. The asthma attacks that had plagued her since childhood always struck when she least wanted attention drawn to herself.

The breathlessness was bad enough, but the wheezing was worse. She had to prevent that at all costs. Her skin was going clammy even as she grabbed for her handbag and wrenched it open. Her hands fumbled with the Ventolin that she always carried with her. It was humiliating to have to spray it into her mouth in front of her father who had taken his place in the passenger seat beside her, but she had no choice, and she gasped in relief as the problem eased.

'I'm sorry, Bernadette,' he said quietly, then sighed. 'I guess I started that. I always seem to cause you distress . . .'

'You had nothing to do with it,' she denied, hating the returning rush of blood that brought a hot flush to her cheeks.

'It's only when you're upset or disturbed that you have an attack,' he reminded her drily. 'The medical reports while you were at school were quite precise, and I don't imagine anything's changed.'

'You don't disturb me. Or upset me,' she

insisted, determined not to give in to him. 'It's probably the smell of the new upholstery in this car. You'd better drive in case the problem comes up again.'

He changed places with her, apologising again as they resettled into the plush lambswool seat-covers which effectively smothered any 'new' smell. But Bernadette noticed that fact too late. The excuse would have to stand now.

'I wish there was something I could do,' her father said, throwing her a look of concern that was surprisingly difficult to rebuff, it seemed so genuine.

'There's nothing,' she retorted sharply. Where had his concern been when she had wanted it . . . needed it?

'I realise that,' he murmured regretfully.

Bernadette was grateful when he dropped the subject and started the car. She didn't want to talk. She needed time to think.

If it was her father who had sent the roses and cards, why had he started them on her nineteenth birthday? It didn't make sense. What could he have intended by them? Was it some subtle form of manipulation . . . to undermine relationships that he didn't deem suitable for her?

But why? Why should he care? What did he want?

And the answer was clear-cut. It couldn't be him. There had to be someone else. Gerard Hamilton certainly had some paternal interest in her—belated though it had been in coming—but he had no time for loving relationships.

Bernadette remembered back to when he had first demonstrated some fatherly concern for her. She had been thirteen, and it was during her first term at an extremely expensive boarding-school—though not the one Alicia had attended. That had been aimed more at social status than the academic achievement prized by the school where Bernadette had been sent. But her fellow students were from privileged families and they knew who she was.

The teasing had been nasty—as nasty as children could make it. Bernadette didn't take kindly to being called a bastard, and she fought back with all her strength. One particular incident landed her in the headmistress's office and Gerard Hamilton was sent for.

Bernadette had not expected him to come, but he had. 'Would you like to change schools, Bernadette?' he had asked.

'I hardly think there would be any point, Father,' she had replied scornfully. '*You* are known everywhere.'

'I could take you to England, if you'd feel happier in another country.'

'No, thank you.' Her chin had lifted in proud defiance. 'No one is going to make me run away.'

He had stared at her for a long moment, and then a semblance of a smile had crossed his face.

At the end of that year he had taken her overseas with him for the whole of January, visiting France and Italy, giving her a visual education that no books could ever supply. It was the first time he had ever spent more than a few hours with her and, while Bernadette would not let herself like him for it, she had learnt to respect the man for the remarkable person he was.

Every January from then on he took her somewhere: Canada and the United States; Switzerland and Austria; Greece and Israel and Egypt; Great Britain and Ireland; Japan and Hong Kong; each year until she was eighteen, when she announced she was going to study medicine and wouldn't have the time to accompany him any more.

He had given that same odd semblance of a smile at that declaration too.

Bernadette wished she knew how his mind ticked. He gave so little away. Nothing that she could really get a hold of. 'What have you been up to lately?' she asked, careful to make the tone of the question as offhand as possible.

'Trying to buy an island,' he answered drily.

'Your own little empire?' she mocked.

He gave that soft laugh that told her she had got him wrong. 'No. If Marlon Brando can own one, there is no reason why I shouldn't as well. I plan to do the same thing and turn it into a holiday resort.'

Bernadette thought that Marlon Brando's island was near Tahiti, but surely her father did not intend to go so far afield? She knew he had a financial interest in several resorts on the Gold

Coast of Queensland.

'Somewhere along the Great Barrier Reef?' she asked, more to have her judgement confirmed than out of curiosity.

He smiled, pleased to be able to surprise her. 'No. One of the smaller Society Islands near Tahiti. It's called Te Enata—the land of men.'

Bernadette raised a sardonic eyebrow. 'And they don't mind you taking it from them?'

He laughed. 'There's only one man concerned. The island is already privately owned. It belongs to Danton Fayette.'

Bernadette caught her breath as her heart kicked an extra beat. Danton Fayette!

The name instantly conjured up the man, the memory so sharp and vivid that it blotted everything else out of her mind: the lean grace of his tall physique; the expressive use of his hands; the fascination of his face that had more to do with the intelligence behind it than the Don Juan good looks; and those wicked, wicked black eyes that flirted and teased and probed and would have swallowed her up if she had weakened to his compelling attraction.

'You met him once in Hong Kong,' her father remarked, then added, as if it was of no consequence at all, 'But it was a long time ago. You may not remember.'

'I remember him,' she muttered tightly, straining to keep her churning emotion under control.

She had hated Danton Fayette . . . and been

fascinated by him. Never before or since had she
been so stirred by a man. He had playfully mocked
all her ambitions and ideals which she had
passionately defended. He had tried to belittle her
beliefs and she had fought him with every weapon
in her armoury. And she was quite certain she had
scored some telling hits. At least she had wiped that
cynical glint from his eyes a few times.

'He remembers you. He asked after you today,'
her father said conversationally.

'I probably gave him a few things to remember
me for,' she said on a note of savage pride.

Gerard Hamilton shot her a sharp look, but
Bernadette made no further comment. Her face
had that closed look that effectively shut him out.
He wondered if there had been more to that
encounter with Danton Fayette than he had seen at
the time.

He hadn't liked the amount of attention Danton
had paid to Bernadette. Nor the way he had looked
at her or danced with her. She had been so young
then—just out of school—no match for an
experienced man of the world like Danton Fayette;
particularly one who was such a practised charmer
and so damnably good-looking; with the added
attraction of a mind that could twist anything to
his advantage.

Certainly nothing had happened that night. And
surely nothing had happened on the ensuing days
either? He would have noticed some change in
Bernadette's pattern of behaviour if Danton had
tried anything, and it had held steady. Danton

could not have pursued her. Or Bernadette had slapped a rejection in his face.

He smiled to himself. That was possible—who knew her sense of resolution better than he? And the thought of his very strong-minded daughter rejecting the sophisticated advances of Danton Fayette gave Gerard considerable amusement as he drove through the city traffic.

Bernadette's thoughts had swung off on another tangent altogether, although Danton Fayette was very much on her mind.

Hong Kong had been six years ago.

'How little you know of life,' he had taunted when she had accused him of pursuing goals that were for his own aggrandisement . . . money and power for the sake of wielding it . . . and women, of course. Bernadette had recognised his type instantly. Danton Fayette was just like her father.

He had pursed his lips in that affected but oddly tantalising manner. 'I wonder if your ideals will still hold their shine in a few years' time. I am tempted to play the devil's advocate . . .' He had paused, then slowly shook his head. 'Curiously enough, with you I'd rather not.'

But Danton Fayette did have the kind of diabolical mind that could conceive such a game as sending those cards and roses. Except his interest in her had only lasted that one night, Bernadette reminded herself cuttingly. She had seen him the next day with a glamorous woman on his arm and he had given Bernadette a mocking little salute in passing.

On to the next game . . . and more compliant prey, Bernadette had thought, and quickly and quietly buried the hurt she felt. Hurt pride, she told herself. His attention had been flattering—and she had not been immune to his compelling attraction—but it was perfectly obvious that he preferred women who didn't challenge what he chose to do with his life.

Or else she wasn't attractive enough to hold his attention. A man like that . . .

The memory stirred an uncomfortable feeling and it took Bernadette several moments to recollect herself and resume a cool-headed reappraisal of her earlier speculation.

It couldn't be Danton Fayette behind the cards and the roses. A man who had discarded his interest in her after one night would hardly be hounding her for six years!

All the same, she wished she could meet Danton Fayette again. She would like very much to match her wits against that clever, cynical mind of his now that she had more years of experience behind her.

She wondered if he was still so wickedly handsome . . . so dangerously sexy . . . or if years of decadence had diminished his magnetic attraction. It would be interesting . . . just to see.

CHAPTER THREE

BERNADETTE snapped out of her introspection as her father turned the Mercedes into the car park beneath the Hotel Inter-Continental. It was one of Sydney's newest hotels and it had the unique architectural feature of having incorporated one of the city's historic landmarks in its structure—the old Treasury building. Bernadette liked the atmosphere of a bygone era that had been created within the confines of a very modern hotel, and could not help feeling pleased that they were dining here tonight.

The car was taken over by attendants. Bernadette and her father took the lift up to the ground floor. They walked along the colonnaded concourse that ran the four sides of a huge open quadrangle. Above it—all three storeys of the Treasury Building—was a sky-lighted roof through which sunlight streamed during the day. A huge urn, resplendant with Australian flora, was the centrepiece of the Cortile. Around it were table settings with comfortable cane armchairs where guests could relax for light snacks or cocktails.

Gerard Hamilton did not pause in his step. He led Bernadette around the Cortile to the Treasury Restaurant, a magnificent high-ceilinged room, furnished with all the formal elegance of a Victorian mansion. All the waiters were in tails, the tables graced with the best of white linen and fine china; and the armchairs around them were upholstered in a beautifully patterned tapestry.

Bernadette smiled in appreciation as she was seated with elaborate courtesy by the head waiter.

'Better now?' her father asked, eyeing her sharply from across the table.

'Fine, thank you.'

Champagne was poured into their glasses. Gerard Hamilton lifted his in a toast. 'To you, my dear, and may you savour every year ahead of you.'

'Thank you, Father,' she said smoothly. 'I intend to, in my own way.'

He smiled. 'What do you plan to do, now that you've finished your internship at the hospital?'

Bernadette shrugged. 'I'll take on a locum for a while . . . get some experience of general practice.'

He nodded approvingly.

Bernadette hesitated over telling him the full truth, then decided he might as well know it now. 'I intend to apply for missionary work. That's what I want to do.'

'That might be dangerous,' he remarked blandly, aware that any sign of disapproval from him might act as a spur to firm her decision, simply to defy his wishes.

Bernadette shrugged, but her eyes held his steadily as she replied, 'I want to take care of the people who can't pay for what they need, who don't have anyone to turn to for help and comfort in their pain. I'm sure you understand that, Father.'

'It's a fine ambition, Bernadette,' he said, understanding all too well what she was telling him. She would give what he had failed to give. But there had to be some way around it. Be damned if he would see her sent to some godforsaken hole! He could pull some strings . . . maybe even block her application . . . but if she found out it would alienate her further. He would have to give it some thought.

The menus were handed to them and conversation was deferred while they made their choices and gave the order.

'Alicia has planned a masked ball for New Year's Eve,' Gerard said in a deliberate change of subject. 'Will you come this year?' He knew what Bernadette's answer would be, but there was always the outside chance that she might change her mind one day.

There were some things he owed her as a father, Bernadette figured, and she kept rigidly to the lines she had drawn up in her mind. They were very basic . . . the provision of a roof over her head and a living allowance until her education was completed. That was what she would have had by birthright if he had married her mother.

Apart from accepting his support until she was capable of supporting herself, Bernadette went out with her father because it was a public acknowledgement of her kinship with him, and she would not be denied that, although nothing he did now could ever make up for the years he had stayed away from her.

But the line stopped at entering the house where his other children had held pride of place all their lives. That was their home . . . never hers. And she wanted no part of it.

'I'm sure a masked ball will be a social *tour de force*,' she remarked lightly. 'But it's not my kind of thing, Father.'

'I would welcome you.'

'I'd hate to steal any of Alicia's thunder.'

'Alicia is currying favour with me at the moment. She'd even give up star-status if it meant a chance that I'd approve her choice of second husband. Plus a generous marriage allowance,' he said with a cynical twist.

'And will you?'

Alicia had left her first husband after four months, declaring him impossible to live with. She was four years older than Bernadette and she had resumed her position as head of her father's house. Gerard had never installed his mistresses in his family home.

He shrugged. 'He wants finance more than he wants Alicia, but he's a better bet than the high-class wimp she chose last time. Who knows? I might get some grandchildren out of it.'

Bernadette bridled at his hard cynicism. 'Don't you care that she'll probably get hurt?'

He looked at her with the weariness of past

experience. 'It's what she wants, Bernadette. If she doesn't know what she's taking on, it's most likely she doesn't want to know. If I tell her, she'll only think I'm trying to destroy her one chance at happiness.'

His eyes twinkled into amused challenge. 'Come . . . you tell me what I should do. And I'll do it.'

He was serious. It surprised Bernadette. The knowledge that it was possible she held the fate of her half-sister in her hands made her pause to consider the problem more deeply before answering.

'If you gave him the finance he wants—no strings attached—and he still wanted Alicia . . .' Bernadette began.

Gerard Hamilton raised a sceptical eyebrow. 'And if he takes the money and leaves, she'll think I bought him off. And hate me for it.' He looked at Bernadette with curious speculation. 'Do you want Alicia to hate me?'

'No.'

Her reply was so spontaneous that Gerard could not doubt its sincerity. He was pleased that her hatred did not extend that far. 'What you suggest . . . I would do that for you, Bernadette, because you have the strength of character to turn away from such a man. Alicia, on the other hand, does not see beyond her emotional desires of the moment.'

'I don't need you to prove a suitor's sincerity to me, Father. I have my own ways and means,'

Bernadette informed him, with a trace of her own bitterly learnt cynicism.

He nodded at the confirmation of her character, and felt a fierce satisfaction. His son was a dilettante, his other daughter a superficial socialite; but Bernadette was of the same fibre as himself. And one day he would hand his empire over to her. He hoped he would be able to see what she made of it.

'As for Alicia,' she said slowly, 'I don't know enough of her to make a fair judgement. I leave it to you. No doubt you have her best interests at heart.'

He ignored the subtle taunt. One day she might understand. When she was older . . . if he lived long enough . . . if his heart didn't give out before he could close the gap between them. He would have to take better care of himself. Do what the doctor told him.

'There are no best interests where Alicia is concerned,' he said tiredly. 'All I can do is keep the peace. And leave the door open for her.'

He paused, wondering if he could plant a receptive seed in Bernadette's mind that might bear fruit some time in the future. He decided it was worth a try. 'My door is always open to you, Bernadette, should you ever care to step over the threshold you've drawn.'

Her eyes glittered at him. 'I didn't draw it, Father.'

'No. But the offer has been there for you to take . . . when you want to,' he reminded her quietly.

Only since his wife had died . . . not during the first twelve years of Bernadette's life. And he could have come to see her before that. He could have been a part-time father to her throughout her childhood.

The couple who had looked after her had never pretended to be her parents, never given her the love she had missed out on by not being part of a normal family. Bernadette had grasped from a very early age that they were paid minders. She had been told that her mother had died soon after giving birth to her, and her father was busy elsewhere. She couldn't remember exactly when she had learnt that he had another family. The sense of being an outcast went back a long way.

And one day, when she was twelve years old, he had simply come to claim a possession he hadn't valued at all while his wife had been alive. Bernadette had defied his right to her with all the pent-up resentment of not ever having belonged to anyone.

'I don't want to live with you. And I won't!' she had cried. 'Don't try to make me. I won't go!'

He hadn't tried to make her. Perhaps he realised she could never feel she belonged there. She didn't belong anywhere. And while he had fulfilled a limited father-role over the last twelve years, she could never feel at home with him, let alone in his house.

She put on a brittle smile. 'It's a bit late for that, don't you think, Father?'

'That's up to you, my dear,' he answered easily, removing any sense of pressure.

Their attention was drawn by the entrance of a noisy party into the subdued atmosphere of the restaurant; a number of men preceded by five stunning-looking women, dressed and groomed in the height of fashion—probably models, Bernadette thought—and all laughing at something that one of the men had said, it seemed, because they were turned towards him with expressions of delighted amusement and happy expectation.

'Danton Fayette,' Gerard muttered in a tone of vexation.

Bernadette's head jerked back to face her father as her heart performed a most uncharacteristic flutter. Even at this distance in time Danton Fayette had an effect on her that no other man had ever had. She felt her heart start to race and sternly took control of herself.

The last thing she would want was for Danton to catch her looking at him with any interest or curiosity. Not after what had happened before. That one time so long ago . . . how close she had come to making a fool of herself! That wouldn't happen again!

If he passed their table, an idle glance at him was acceptable, but she would not allow the feelings he aroused in her to show in any way . . . to betray even the slightest hint of her vulnerability to his potent attraction.

She was prickly with awareness of the party's progress towards them. She hoped that it would not stop short of where she and her father were seated, so that she could see the man again without appearing overtly curious.

Bernadette worked on perfecting a façade of indifference as the voices came closer and closer . . .

'You must come, Danton . . .'

'Danton, darling . . .'

'Danton, you couldn't possibly . . .'

How typical that he should have gathered a harem of beautiful women about him, Bernadette thought savagely. The other men in the party obviously didn't count. The women only had eyes for him! If ever there was a satyr of a man, it was Danton Fayette! To have even considered for a moment that he might have sent the cards and the roses was utter madness. His whole attitude to the female sex was diametrically opposed to such constancy.

'Gerard . . .'

The low, sexy drawl struck an instant chord of memory and vibrated along it, making Bernadette's nerves tingle with tension.

The waiter leading the party glanced back at Danton, who gave directions in his smooth, charming manner. 'Please take my guests on to our table and see to their needs. I'll be with you all in a moment or two.'

'Please don't leave your guests,' her father said in reluctant acknowledgement as the man halted beside them.

'Pardon me for intruding, Gerard . . .'

A shiver of apprehension ran through her body . . . or was it anticipation? The quick rise and fall of her breasts . . . she hoped he hadn't noticed. Bernadette clamped her fingers together, nails pressing tightly into her flesh under cover of the tablecloth. The need to prevent any revealing reaction to him was paramount. Control was the only key to handling a man like Danton Fayette.

She repressed the nervous flutter of emptiness that attacked her stomach and commanded herself to relax . . . at least externally. Only then did she lift her head—slowly—her eyes dragging up the tall, lean physique of the man—elegantly clothed in a dinner-suit. Her gaze lingered briefly on the darkly tanned throat—she knew now that he would be just as she remembered him—the sharply chiselled chin, the sensual mouth with its knowing little curve, the aristocratic nose.

She steeled herself to look once more into those disturbingly magnetic black eyes. As soon as she did so, she knew it was a mistake. They still had their power to draw and hold her, probing into her soul, raking her heart for desires that had to be sternly repressed.

Six years had gone by. But it might have been yesterday when she last saw him. The black curly hair was as riotous as ever, lending its emphasis to the rakish arch of his eyebrows, and the thickly lashed eyes held the same wicked taunt, as if he knew everything and was amused by it all.

Yet there was something different.

It took Bernadette a moment to realise what it was. The world-weariness that had been carved into the lines around his eyes and mouth was no longer so apparent. Not apparent at all. His face radiated an inner vitality, an excitement with life, and it made him more electrically handsome, impossible to ignore.

He flashed her a dazzling white smile. 'You must forgive me. The temptation to reacquaint myself with your very beautiful daughter was simply too great to resist.'

Bernadette couldn't contain a slight flush of pleasure. He did remember her. And found her attractive. He even wished to renew their acquaintance.

But Gerard Hamilton was annoyed. The sense of having been manipulated by Danton Fayette niggled at the edge of his mind. This meeting was not coincidental. But what was Danton aiming at? Why was he hedging over the deal Gerard had offered him? There were few men whose minds Gerard could not read, and Danton Fayette was one of them. Which made any negotiation with him a very tricky business.

And he didn't like the way he was smiling at Bernadette, either! 'The bevy of beauty you brought in with you is surely enough distraction for one night, Danton,' he mocked. 'Be satisfied with what you've got.'

'Ah, Gerard . . .' The black eyes glanced lazily at him and a light laugh rippled from his throat. 'You are jealous of this daughter! I thought as much.'

A sense of danger prickled along Gerard's spine. He forced himself to smile. 'Bernadette is very much her own woman.'

'So she would have me believe,' Danton said whimsically, then turned back to Bernadette. His body seemed to tighten like a spring that could suddenly and lethally uncoil, but his voice was lazy and remote. 'Six years ago. The Mandarin Hotel. Hong Kong. You were a very young eighteen and determined on a career in medicine, as I recall.'

Very young indeed, she agreed privately, but a match for him even then, she thought with pride. And pride kept her face as smooth as alabaster, her eyes bland pools of indifference as she replied to the lightly flicking sting in his words.

'Yes. As a matter of fact, I'm a fully qualified doctor now,' she informed him coolly, then with more bite, 'What have you been doing with yourself, Danton? If I remember correctly, your ideas on life were over-refined and positively . . . sensual! Our aims and goals were totally opposed. Did you achieve what you set out to achieve?'

The smile lurked at the corners of his mouth as his lips formed a little movement which suggested consideration and a lot of other things besides. He was without a doubt the most compelling man that Bernadette had ever encountered. Despite the exertions of her considerable will-power, he could still make her pulse race as madly as it had raced when she was a teenager.

'No. But I approximate it more closely with every year, with every day. I will not fail,' he said, and for once there seemed to be a serious gleam in his eyes.

'So I see, by the company you keep tonight,' she mocked.

He laughed. 'Entrancing, aren't they? And so eager! It's the price one pays for success!' His eyes glittered between mockery and sheer devilry. 'But I'm sure you will not be over-flattered when I say you would be . . . at least as enchanting. To the right man.'

'To the right man, yes!' Gerard cut in, determined on spiking this particular by-play. His instincts were picking up the current running between Danton and Bernadette and he didn't trust the man . . . not with his daughter. 'But definitely not one who's fond of collecting pets for his amusement,' he drawled with a nod towards the table where Danton's guests had been seated.

Gerard saw the slight stiffening of Bernadette's spine and hoped it was enough. Hate him she might, but it was safer for her if she hated Danton Fayette too.

'A very tactless statement, Gerard. And untrue,' Danton mocked, and the glitter in his black eyes gave warning of battle.

Gerard silently applauded the light laugh Bernadette gave—an easy ripple of amusement.

'And who—in your opinion—would be the right man for me, Danton?' she asked. Not him—her father was right about that—but still she could not resist challenging the man . . . holding his attention a little while longer.

He waved his hand dismissively. 'How much have you changed in the years since I first saw you?'

'Not at all!'

The eyebrows expressed scepticism. 'I would wish to judge for myself.'

'That would probably be extremely boring for me.' She gave him a slow, confident smile. 'I'm the one who is serious about life, Danton. You are the one who plays at it. Remember? So take your chance now. You won't get another.'

'Why not? I'll be attending your father's masked ball on New Year's Eve.' His eyebrows lifted sardonically. 'Or are you still the frightened little girl who fears to go into her father's mansion . . . because she might get hurt?'

'That's enough, Danton!' Gerard grated, furious with the man's crude counter-stroke. 'I won't have you or anyone else insulting my daughter. I'd be obliged if you . . .'

'Don't be ridiculous, Father!' Bernadette snapped, the words spitting from an upsurge of fiery pride. She didn't need him to stand up for her. She could do it herself. Particularly where Danton Fayette was concerned! 'Danton is merely trying to needle me . . . in a very amateurish fashion, I might add.' She raised a mocking eyebrow at Danton. 'You seem to have lost all your subtlety. Definitely boring.'

He gave a soft throaty laugh. 'I guarantee you will not be bored, Bernadette. I'll make a point of keeping you on your toes. I shall also be fascinated to see what costume you wear.'

She almost said she was not going, but she held the words back, looking consideringly at Danton. She didn't like the thought that people might be interpreting her decision to stay away from her father's home as weakness of character . . . even cowardice!

On the other hand, Danton might be using the unpalatable suggestion to manipulate her . . . to stir her into accepting his challenge, as he had with the dancing in Hong Kong. This time she would act on her will, not react to his!

'And what costume would you wear, Danton? Let me guess,' she drawled, her eyes telegraphing that he was all too predictable.

His mouth made that provocatively sensual movement again. 'That will be my first surprise. One among many.'

Bernadette's mind moved into high gear. Sometimes a principle had to be changed in order to meet the demands of an even higher one; and if people did think it was out of fear that she stayed away . . . maybe she should go to the ball. If she did, she would have the opportunity of knocking Danton Fayette back on his heels again.

'Perhaps I don't care to wear a mask,' she said, careful not to give away her thoughts. Let him wonder, she thought with secret satisfaction. She wasn't about to make anything easy for him.

'Or could it be that you've worn one too long, and you're frightened of what's beneath it?' he taunted.

Gerard bit down on his tongue. However much he disliked what was going on, he had to let Bernadette handle it by herself. To interfere any more might drive her Danton's way. He sat back and watched in poker-faced silence.

Bernadette laughed, to show Danton he couldn't goad her into doing what he wanted. But she could not deny the exhilaration of matching wits with him. He was a rogue, but an endlessly tantalising one . . . and he challenged her in a way no other man ever had. Why not rise to that challenge and prove him as contemptible as the others who had aspired to use her for their own purposes?

At least he wasn't fortune-hunting. As long as she kept her head—and of course she would—the idea of humbling Danton Fayette was more intoxicating than any wine.

'The truth is . . . I don't live in fear of anything, Danton,' she said in a bored tone. 'I simply find you insufferable.'

The insult amused him. 'You told me that once before. And I didn't believe you then. We danced too well together, Bernadette.'

The memory burned through her mind. He had held her so close, made her feel terribly aware of his body, and her own. But she had been much younger then . . . inexperienced.

'I'm not as interested in frivolous activities as you are,' she said scornfully.

'Indeed?' His eyes twinkled wickedly. 'Then let me offer you a contest in character. I will unmask you . . . see your true identity . . . before you can detect mine.'

'It's no contest. I'd know you anywhere. There is no mask you can hide behind.'

His smile was teasingly confident. 'We shall see who is right . . . and wrong. I look forward to our next encounter. It should be . . . very illuminating.'

He turned to Gerard, who had listened to every nuance of the conversation with growing unease, although he did not allow it to show on his face. He suspected that Danton Fayette had just played a new card in the poker-game he had been playing for the last two weeks, and Gerard wasn't sure what it meant. He sensed there was a new dimension to this business. Perhaps he wasn't buying an island at all. Perhaps he was unintentionally selling his daughter. All he knew was that he didn't like it.

The black eyes of his adversary gleamed with satisfaction. 'I won't interrupt your evening any further, Gerard . . . Bernadette. I hope you both enjoy your dinner.'

'Thank you. And you, too,' Gerard replied with flat politeness, but his mind was furiously working on all the possibilities.

Danton flashed his smile at them and departed.

Bernadette watched him stroll on to the table where his 'pets' had been seated. A contest with Danton Fayette—one that she would win—was very, very tempting! She would show him! And everyone else who thought she couldn't face up to the possibility of being hurt by her father's family!

However, to go to the ball was also a concession to her father's wishes, and she didn't like that. Not one bit. The turnabout from her resolute refusals of any invitation to his home might make him think she was softening. She told herself again that she didn't care what her father thought of her, but she was very conscious of his watching eyes as she flicked her gaze back to him. A most unwelcome flush crept into her cheeks.

And Gerard Hamilton knew in that instant how very dangerous his adversary was. 'You intend to come to the ball, Bernadette?' he asked, struggling to hide his disbelief and chagrin that Danton Fayette should achieve the breakthrough that he himself had so dearly wanted to make.

'You said you wanted me to come,' she replied with a touch of her old defiance. 'Perhaps one has to start somewhere. This could be the time.'

Gerard grew even more uneasy, in a way he had never envisaged. The first step taken into his house could be the start of other things . . . the ice broken at last . . . but Danton Fayette was such an unpredictable element!

He frowned. 'Please don't mistake what I say now, because you will always be welcome, Bernadette . . .'

He searched hard for the right words. Bernadette might not need protecting, but the urge to protect was too intense to put aside.

'Danton Fayette is the most dangerous man I know,' he said with measured seriousness. 'And I do not say that lightly, Bernadette.' His eyes swept hers in sharp warning. 'He's playing a game. And Danton doesn't play to any ordinary rules. He always keeps hidden cards up his sleeve until he wishes to reveal them . . . and when he does . . .' He shook his head. 'If you can beat him, Bernadette, you're a better man than I am.'

The words slipped out—his concern for her blurring his mind—and he knew the moment he had spoken them that he had made a terrible mistake. He saw the resolution firming in Bernadette's eyes and cursed himself for underlining the challenge.

'I can play any game, Father. Just like you,' she said with steely pride. 'Even if I have to invent the rules as I go along.'

She would show them! Both Danton and her father! For the first time in her life she would step inside her father's house . . . and if either man attempted to manipulate her in any way, for any purpose whatsoever, she would demonstrate beyond a shadow of a doubt that she was her own woman! And beholden to no one!

CHAPTER FOUR

BERNADETTE searched the costume and theatrical agencies that provided fancy dress for hire, but there was nothing that struck her eye as *right*. She didn't want anything hackneyed or obvious. Whatever she wore to the masked ball had to be a challenge to Danton Fayette, a statement that expressed something positive, yet did not give her identity away.

Eventually she worked out an idea that held a piquancy of purpose that satisfied her, but to have it made up was a problem. The designers and society dressmakers who could take on such a job were inclined to gossip about what they had made for their patrons. If word got out—and she wouldn't put it past Danton to cheat by trying to learn what she would wear—then it would be no genuine contest.

But for once luck smiled on her.

She sold the Mercedes sports car and presented the proceeds to the women's shelter, insisting that some of the money be used to make the place more cosy and cheerful. One of the women who had sought refuge there was happy to make curtains and cushions—anything to get her mind off her wretched personal problems.

When Bernadette admired her skilled workmanship, the woman offered the information that she had once worked in a designer's factory and knew all the professional tricks of making up quality clothes and furnishings. She was delighted at the generous proposition Bernadette put to her, and quite excited about making the costume and mask, elaborating on Bernadette's idea with all the enthusiasm of someone doing something really creative.

With that problem solved, Bernadette decided to take on a job as a locum. There were lots of positions on offer, since many doctors wanted to get away on holiday at this time of year. Bernadette found the wide experience of general practice more interesting and less pressurised than her previous hospital work.

She was kept busy, but not so rushed that she didn't have time to chat to her patients, and she liked that. Very much. She wanted to help people in more than a strictly medical sense. She wanted to reassure them, make them feel better. She knew all too well what it was like not to have someone who would listen . . . and care.

Christmas came. Gerard Hamilton presented Bernadette with a magnificent pearl necklace and matching ear-rings. Bernadette gave him a small but exquisitely dainty Lladro figurine of a mermaid.

'If you're still buying the Te Enata island, I'd hate to think there wasn't something female around your "land of men",' she commented drily, embarrassed by his obvious pleasure in the gift. It was the first time she had given her father something that didn't proclaim itself a 'duty' gift.

The truth was, she felt vaguely guilty about going to the masked ball because of Danton. No matter what other reasons she used to bolster her decision, she knew they were of relatively minor consideration, and it seemed just a little two-faced to have refused her father's invitations to his home all these years, and then go because Danton had chosen that venue for their duel. It had made her feel . . . mean . . . and she hadn't liked the feeling.

Gerard Hamilton frowned. 'Danton keeps displaying interest in our offer for the island, but he hasn't declared himself openly . . . yet! He's waiting for something. And I don't know what.'

He looked across at Bernadette, and again that crawly sense of danger wriggled down Gerard's spine. What was Danton waiting for . . . and why did he have this feeling that Bernadette was involved with it? He made a conscious effort to relax.

'Since the Mercedes is gone, I'll send my car for you on New Year's Eve,' he said with an encouraging smile. 'Alicia and Alex are looking forward to meeting you.'

'It should be interesting,' she said glibly, doubting the sincerity of her half-sister and half-brother. She could not imagine they would truly be in favour of having a cuckoo in the nest. After all, they could have come and met her at any time in the last twelve years if they had really been interested in her.

Her smile hid her thoughts. 'And thank you for the offer of the car, Father. I accept.' Since she was going to her father's home, she would go in the same style that was available to Alicia and Alex.

Gerard Hamilton tried another invitation. 'Why not join us for Christmas dinner, Bernadette? It would make . . .'

'I'm afraid that's impossible, Father,' she interrupted, smoothly and decisively. 'I'm on call for the surgery where I'm working at the moment. All day.'

And that was that! But Gerard carried some satisfaction away with him. Her gift of the mermaid figurine—the thought . . . the impulse behind it—was the first crack in twelve years of ice.

The next six days passed quickly for Bernadette, speeded along by a growing sense of exhilarating anticipation. Her costume and mask were finished and she was absolutely thrilled with the effect created. Her mind was endlessly teased by what Danton might choose to wear, and she amused herself thinking up various lines she could say when she unmasked him!

Faust . . . Mephistopheles . . . Casanova . . . Rasputin . . . those were the identities that suited his character, but Bernadette didn't underestimate his deviousness. He would be out to trick her, but she was certain she would know him as soon as she saw him. Danton Fayette was far too distinctive a personality for him to escape her eye.

Bernadette had the day off work on New Year's Eve. She went to her hairdresser and had lighter streaks put through her dark blonde hair. The long tresses were softly curled and allowed to flow free. The effect was precisely what she wanted.

When it finally came time to dress for the ball, Bernadette was almost bubbling with excitement. The skirt of her costume was an artistic masterpiece: handkerchief drifts of chiffon graduating upwards from black and midnight purple to a mauve-grey with hints of palest pink and lemon nearing the waistline. The seed pearls and mother-of-pearl sequins on the sculptured belt picked up these shades and threw them up to the white strapless bodice which was gathered into a sunray pattern of tiny pleats.

The pearls her father had given her for Christmas were a perfect accompaniment to her costume and it also seemed fitting to wear them as a gesture of good will. Bernadette still felt uncomfortable about taking up her father's invitation when she knew her acceptance had nothing to do with a conciliatory meeting on his home ground.

She shook off the feeling and concentrated on positioning the mask correctly. It half covered her face and was fitted to a crown-like head-dress which featured five star-like points spread across the top of her head from ear to ear, creating the pictorial image of a pale sun rising and glittering with the same sequins and seed-pearls that were on her belt. The mask openings for her eyes were similarly decorated, achieving a wonderfully exotic effect.

Bernadette grinned happily at her reflection in the mirror. *Comes the dawn* . . . for Danton Fayette. She would show him the light, if he tried to work any of his dark designs on her. She laughed in sheer exuberance at the contest ahead of her. He would never recognise her in this mask, and with her hair done so differently.

She almost danced out of her bedroom to answer the doorbell when it rang, and could not help smiling when her father's chauffeur looked stunned at her appearance.

'Miss Bernadette . . .' He shook his head, momentarily speechless.

'Will I do, Jeffrey?' she asked, and twirled around for him.

The chauffeur was a kindly man who had been in her father's employ for over thirty years. He had driven her to boarding-school on her first day there, and had always shown a friendly interest in her.

'You'll be belle of the ball, Miss Bernadette,' he declared warmly. 'I reckon Mr Hamilton will be bursting to show you off to everyone.'

'That's not what I want, Jeffrey,' she said drily.

The old chauffeur sighed. 'Only natural,' he muttered. 'You don't know how proud he is of you, Miss Bernadette.'

Proud? Bernadette queried in her mind. He

hadn't been proud enough to even acknowledge her as a child. But perhaps it was different now, and there was some pride in her. Why else did he persist in being part of her life, and wanting her to be part of his?

She locked her apartment and accompanied the chauffeur down to her father's Rolls-Royce. It was not a long drive from her apartment block at Bondi Beach to the famed mansion—Huntingdon—at Point Piper. Bernadette had often wondered if Gerard Hamilton had bought the place because its name was so similar in sound to his own, or simply because it was an affirmation of his vast wealth.

The mansion had been built at the end of the last century and was certainly one of the most prestigious and expensive private residences in Sydney, set as it was on harbour-front acreage and requiring more than a few servants to maintain the place in its full glory.

Jeffrey cruised the Rolls along at a sedate pace. He suddenly cleared his throat and glanced over his shoulder to draw Bernadette's attention.

'May I say, Miss Bernadette, how very pleased I am that you're coming home at last. Even if it is only for tonight.'

'Thank you, Jeffrey. But it doesn't really mean anything, you know.'

'It's been a long time,' he said with a note of sadness. 'Maybe I shouldn't say this . . . I know you've got reason to be hard on your father, Miss Bernadette, but . . . he's getting on in years. You shouldn't forget that. Better to make your peace with him before . . . well, before anything happens.'

Bernadette frowned over the implications of the chauffeur's advice, knowing it was well-meant. 'Is there something wrong with my father, Jeffrey?'

'Now I didn't say that, Miss Bernadette,' he answered hurriedly. 'I just know how pleased he is about you coming to Huntingdon. I hope you have a good time tonight. Maybe you'll want to come back soon.'

'Maybe,' she said non-committally.

The chauffeur fell silent again and Bernadette mused over what he had said. Her father was only fifty-eight years old and still looked in his prime. She had at least another twenty years to 'make her peace with him', if she ever did. Let him justify what he had done to her first, she thought bitterly. He had never even tried!

The Rolls turned into the arched gateway to Huntingdon and slowed to a crawl as it followed other cars ahead of it. Guests were arriving in a steady stream. The three-storey sandstone mansion was lit by spotlights from the landscaped gardens, impressive for sheer size if not for elegant architecture. The entrance portico was supported by massive columns which rose majestically to the second storey. The house looked more like a museum than a home, Bernadette thought, and she was glad she didn't live in it.

The Rolls pulled up at the front steps. A car attendant opened her door and helped Bernadette out. The guests ahead of her turned to look back

and stared quizzically at her before proceeding into
the reception foyer. Bernadette smiled to herself,
sure that her identity could not be probed. She
joined the line being greeted by a sheikh—all too
obviously Gerard Hamilton—who had a harem girl
positioned on one side of him and Madame
Pompadour on the other.

Not even her father recognised her. He glanced
down at the invitation card she handed him.

'You know why I'm here,' she said quickly and
quietly, recalling the chauffeur's surmise that
Gerard would want to parade her around. 'I wish
to remain incognito, except to the family.'

'I have already ensured that you will. Danton
will get no help from me,' he said grimly, then
smiled. 'The pearls look well on you.'

'Thank you.'

He touched Madame Pompadour's arm, drawing
her attention from the previous party of arrivals to
Bernadette. 'Alicia . . . this is our special guest.'

She offered a hand and a slightly stiff smile.
'Welcome to Huntingdon. I hope you enjoy the
evening's festivities.' The words were consciously
gracious. 'I hope to catch up with you after the
unmasking at midnight.'

'Yes. Thank you,' Bernadette murmured, finding it
oddly difficult to match her half-sister's composure.

Alicia held on to her hand as she signalled a man
in a Louis the Fourteenth costume. He sauntered
over from the guests he had been welcoming.

'Alex, you'll take our special guest in, won't
you?' Alicia said with pointed emphasis.

'Charmed,' he drawled, and sketched Bernadette an elaborate bow before offering his arm. He was as tall as Gerard, but lean enough to look quite elegant in his period costume.

'Well, well, well,' he half chuckled as he drew Bernadette away from the reception line. 'You do do the old man proud. If you weren't my blood-relation, dear sis, I'd be chatting you up in no time flat.'

'You're not doing a bad job of it right now,' Bernadette retorted drily.

His mouth quirked at one corner. 'I've had my instructions, and it's more than my life's worth to offend you. I do depend on Daddy to keep me in the manner to which I've become accustomed.'

'I thought you'd made a name for yourself as a professional photographer?' Bernadette queried.

He laughed. 'A part-time hobby. My profession is strictly that of playboy. I could never measure up to dear Papa, so I turned my back on the neurosis of trying and failing miserably. It's much more enjoyable for me to spend the money he enjoys making.'

'I see,' Bernadette murmured, barely keeping her contempt for his attitude out of her voice.

'Do you, my lovely?' he mocked. 'Do you see where you fit into the grand design?'

She didn't know what *grand design* he was talking about, but Bernadette was not about to admit that to her feckless half-brother. It was perfectly obvious that Gerard had both Alicia and Alex tied to his will because of his wealth, but not her. Never her!

'I have my own design, Alex,' she said in careless disdain.

'Fascinating,' he drawled. 'However, the plan tonight is for me to whirl you on to the ballroom floor, trot the light fantastic with you until you've had the chance to look over the company, then leave you to your own devices. If that does not meet with your approval, please give me your instructions. I am bidden to do your pleasure.'

'Can you dance well?' Bernadette asked.

'One of the arts a playboy must practise regularly,' he retorted with mock solemnity.

'Then I shall enjoy dancing with you. And thank you, Alex. I'll try not to tread on your toes.'

'Splendid!' he said, and led her into a ballroom that was unbelievably huge and opulent.

It had to be something like thirty metres square, with glass doors at the far end that led on to a vast patio which overlooked the harbour. Fabulous chandeliers hung from the ceiling which was two storeys high, and a balcony ran all around the first floor, overlooking the ballroom below. A magnificent staircase led down from two sides, joined at a central landing, then provided an entrance to the room that was marvellously theatrical.

Alex gestured towards it. 'For the ladies' powder-room you take the right-hand staircase.'

'Thank you,' Bernadette murmured.

The dance-band—set up at the opposite side of the room to the staircase—was playing a jazz-waltz, and Alex swept her around the parquet floor with a lightness of foot that Bernadette found very enjoyable. There were many couples dancing and Bernadette carefully eyed every man that passed by, but not one of them was Danton.

'This music is for the older generation,' Alex remarked drily. 'Another band takes over at eleven, and then we'll have a real beat to hot things up.' His voice dropped to an exasperated mutter. 'Damn! Another one.'

'What's the matter?' Bernadette asked.

He grimaced. 'I do prefer to be an original. We now have three Louis the Fourteenths: me, Alicia's intended for the matrimonial merry-go-round, and some other dog who's just walked in.'

Bernadette smiled to herself, hardly glancing at the newcomer. One thing was certain. Danton Fayette would make sure he was an original.

But one hour passed into another and Bernadette could not spot him anywhere. She danced with several men, and in between dances she casually skirted the whole company of guests in the ballroom and out on the patio, but was completely frustrated in her search. And Alex undoubtedly was even more peeved, since the number of Louis the Fourteenths had grown to at least half a dozen. One of them was sporting a flashy fleur-de-lis brooch in his cravat, an extra nicety that Alex probably wished he had thought of to make himself more distinctive, even if the jewellery was made of paste.

Danton had to be deliberately leaving his arrival late, just to tantalise her. Bernadette decided to make for the powder-room to re-check her appearance. She rearranged her hair then wandered back out to the staircase, pausing at the top step to look down over the crowd. But she saw no one new among the revellers below.

The harem girl was still clinging to Gerard's side . . . had done so all night. Bernadette concluded that she was Tammy Gardner, her father's current mistress who had held his favour for over two years now—longer than most. Bernadette caught herself wondering how long her mother had lasted, and instantly clamped down on the thought.

Where the devil was Danton?

She recalled her father saying that Danton Fayette played to no rule, but Bernadette's patience was running out. She decided to give him a bit of his own medicine, and instead of returning to the ballroom she walked over to the doors that led out to a huge open balcony which obviously roofed the patio below.

The breeze off the harbour was very pleasant. She wished she could take her mask off but didn't dare risk it. She couldn't give Danton that advantage . . . if he came looking for her. He had to be here somewhere. But in what guise? He always played with hidden cards, her father had said.

Bernadette pondered the idea as she wandered over to the balcony railing and gazed out at the city lights on the other side of the harbour, too preoccupied to really see them.

Hidden was the key word. Somehow Danton was hiding his identity from her.

The creaking of a chair startled her and she swung around. One of the Louis the Fourteenths—Alex?—rose lazily from a cane table-setting in the far shadows of the balcony.

'I've been waiting for you, Bernadette.'

Danton's voice! Bernadette was speechless with shock as he strolled forward, his white smile gleaming beneath his mask.

'And I now claim victory,' he said with taunting satisfaction.

CHAPTER FIVE

BERNADETTE burned with frustration. He had beaten her, but not fair and square, in her opinion. 'How long have you been hiding up here, Danton?'

He laughed, a ripple of triumphant amusement. 'Oh, no, my shining light of the world! Do not start making excuses. I'll accept none of them. I pre-empted your move out on to this balcony when you retired to the powder-room. For the rest, I have been in full view since I arrived a couple of hours ago.'

His hand swept out in a mocking gesture of openness. 'I gave you every chance to identify me: danced past you three times; stood openly in groups that you scrutinised; even took a glass of champagne from a waiter's tray at the same time as you did. Your eyes skated over me every time.'

She could not doubt he spoke the truth. His satisfaction at her failure to perceive him was in every taunting word. All she could do was chip away some of his pride in his victory.

'It's clear then that I overestimated you, Danton. I actually believed you were quite individual. To find you are one among many is a bitter disappointment. Not worthy of a contest.'

His smile denied any chagrin at her comments.

'And who, do you suppose, engineered the "many", Bernadette? Believe me, it didn't happen by chance. A word here and there . . . a suggestion . . . a piece of advice. I must admit I cannot claim the idea as original—Edgar Allan Poe hid the letter everyone was looking for in the most obvious place—but it was wonderfully diverting to use it.'

Hidden! Yes, she understood what her father meant now. Danton had been ingeniously clever, doing what he wanted to do, and using other people for his disguise. It was also a sobering demonstration of how easily he could manipulate others to serve his purpose.

'As for individuality,' he drawled. 'I have that, too! I played fairly with you, Bernadette. You simply did not recognise the clue. I am the only Louis the Fourteenth wearing the fleur-de-lis.'

His hand lifted to the ruffled lace of his cravat where the emblem of French heraldry was on ostentatious display, set with magnificent diamonds. Bernadette remembered her eyes flitting over it, dismissing it as a piece of foppery, but if Danton was wearing it those glittering stones would certainly not be paste.

'Quite a few women remarked on it,' he said, pointing up her failure again with obvious relish.

Bernadette had seen enough good jewellery to have some idea what such a piece was worth, and she was appalled at what he had spent on a mere affectation. For one night!

'What a waste of money! That must have cost you a hundred thousand dollars at least,'

Bernadette retorted scornfully.

'As far as I recall, there wasn't any change . . . but then it's worth it to prove a point . . . and I'm sure it will work out as a good investment, anyway.' His mouth pursed slightly in that teasingly sensual way that drew attention to it. 'Have I proved my point now?'

Bernadette still bridled against admitting defeat. 'Is this how you identify yourself, Danton? As the grandiose Sun-King?' she mocked.

Again he laughed. 'French-born, decadent, sinful, vain, extravagant . . . isn't that how you see me, Bernadette? Come now, I was making it easy for you.'

In one sense he was right. But that description placed him on the same level as her half-brother, Alex, and Danton's character was much deeper, far more complex . . . levels and levels of him that she had not yet probed, hardly begun to recognise. It was a disquieting thought, but the evidence for it was overwhelming. He had even somehow used her half-brother to deceive her. It was time to reconsider.

'No. That's not how I see you,' she said quietly and truthfully. He was far more dangerous than that. She was not even sure that Rasputin or Mephistopheles were closer to the mark.

He made no immediate response. His silence and his total lack of any movement created an odd stillness which sent a strange little shiver through her heart.

'Then *you* have changed,' he said softly.

And something in his voice caused the queerest melting feeling inside her. Her mind leapt instantly on to defence, on guard against any form of weakness. 'How absurd!' she scoffed. All her principles and ambitions had not changed one iota from when she had met him six years ago.

He shrugged, then began taking off his mask. 'Your mind was once intensely focused on yourself. Obsessively so.' He lifted off the long, curly wig and placed both wig and mask on the wide stone ledge of the balcony balustrade. 'A fine mind, I thought, but narrowed by circumstance.'

A whimsical smile hovered on his lips as he turned to her, and for once Bernadette saw no taunt in the gleaming black eyes. 'Black and white, Bernadette. But now there is a dawning of awareness . . . a perception of shades . . . and I have won the right to unmask you.'

He was using the subtleties of her own costume as a weapon for himself, yet Bernadette was so bemused by his judgement of her—was it true?—that his last low words didn't sink in until his hands had lifted to her face. She instinctively flinched away from his touch before she could consider what he was doing. Her heart leapt erratically at his nearness and she took a half-step backwards, half lifting an arm to ward him away.

'You don't concede that I won?' he mocked.

'How did you identify me?' she demanded to know, needing time to regain control over what was happening to her. Her mind felt overloaded with confusing impressions, and a frightening sensitivity was sweeping through her body.

'I looked for a woman who stood out from the crowd. There was only one,' he answered simply.

'There were several outstanding costumes,' she argued.

'Only one that you would choose.'

'Why? How did you know?'

'Darkness . . . light. Night . . . day. Sin . . . purity. Evil . . . goodness. Despair . . . hope. You shouted at me, Bernadette. Preached to me. And offered me what I now take.'

'No,' she whispered, appalled that he had read her so easily.

'Yes,' he said in a low, throaty voice, his eyes holding her mesmerised as he lifted off her mask and set it aside on the balustrade. 'To the victor, the spoils.'

His arm swept around her waist and pulled her close, locking her body to his hard strength.

Bernadette's hands flew up in ineffectual protest. 'No,' she cried frantically. 'Only the mask. That's what we agreed on.'

His eyes glittered into hers as the fingers of his other hand threaded through her hair and curled relentlessly around the nape of her neck.

'Bernadette . . . this is the unmasking,' he told her huskily, his head bending slowly towards hers.

And she couldn't evade him. He was too strong. And somehow the enforced contact with his body had seeped all the strength from hers. Her thighs trembled against the muscular power of his. Her stomach quivered in awareness of the masculine contours that the fine chiffon of her skirt and the period hose of his costume did little to smother.

His lips played with hers in a sensual teasing that electrified every nerve-ending in her body, seduced her compliance, and drew a response that broke a barrier of inhibitions that had always protected Bernadette from other predatory men. Her lips parted without any conscious volition and his mouth stole into the intimate territory she had previously guarded, plunging her through a dizzying range of new sensations, drawing her into a wild, erotic excitement that accelerated beyond any semblance of control.

She surrendered to the hard, driving passion of his will, enthralled by the sensations he evoked with his ruthless invasion. Her fingers dug into his shoulders, scrambled upwards and thrust into the thick, wiry curls at the back of his head; clinging, clutching. Her body strained closer, wanting every intimacy of contact.

She barely knew when the kiss ended. Danton's mouth swept over hers as he breathed in hard. 'Even you are not immune to passion, Bernadette. Your kiss is as sweet as the nectar of the gods . . . and much more intoxicating.'

His mouth plunged down again before she could gather her senses into any coherence, the fullness of his lips meeting hers, moulding, soothing, evoking more and more exquisite sensations, whirling her through a different reality where she no longer belonged to herself, where she needed to be fused with him and nothing else mattered.

Then his arms were crushing her body into his and his mouth was brushing over her hair, whispering urgent words. 'You can't fight this, Bernadette. Admit the truth: I excite you as much as you excite me. It's why you came to the ball, why I came . . . and what we both want is to go on from here. So come away with me now. Be with me. We'll plumb the depths of each other . . . know all there is to know . . . in a way no one else has ever done.'

Yes, yes, yes . . . she thought in mad exultation, until sanity jabbed through the thraldom that had held her mindless. The memory of his 'pets' was a swift and savage counter to the temptation he offered, and with that memory came a sobering wave of shame that she had been swept so quickly and so deeply into his power.

And pain: the pain of having her pride in her own autonomy ripped to tatters; the pain of finding herself as vulnerable to this man as any other woman; the pain of knowing that he knew what he could do to her; and pain that sliced into her thumping heart and sprang a steel band around her chest.

Oh, no . . . no, she willed frantically as she struggled for breath. She couldn't have an asthma attack now. Not now! Not in front of him!

But, no matter how hard she willed, the symptoms did not abate. It was going to happen. She couldn't stop it.

She dropped her hands to his shoulders and tried to push away. Her arms were as weak as water. Her body writhed against his embrace. She opened her mouth in a desperate grab for air, but the muscles of her throat had already tightened.

'Bernadette?' He looked down at her in dismay.

She couldn't speak. She heard the awful rattle in her throat and felt the most miserable despair. She hit at him to let her go. His embrace loosened. Bernadette snatched desperately at the small evening-bag that she had hung on her wrist, tore at the pull-string opening, her hand scrabbling for the Ventolin.

Her fingers closed shakily around it and she threw herself out of Danton's arms and turned her heaving back on him as she used it. The ghastly high-pitched wheezing finally died. Tears sprang into her eyes. She couldn't bear to face Danton, not in this hopelessly debilitated condition.

'Please,' she gasped. 'Leave me. I don't want you near me! Not ever again! I think you're the most despicable man I've ever met!'

His hands closed gently around her upper arms and she could feel the warmth emanating from his body right behind her. 'Don't say that!' His voice was low, urgent, demanding her attention. 'I can help you, Bernadette. Believe me. Lots of people suffer from asthma. I'm sorry if I'm the cause of bringing that on, but I didn't know, and it's over now. We must go forward, not retreat back into the past. Our relationship . . .'

'Is over! And so is the contest!' Bernadette punched out with as much vehement force as she could manage.

If he thought he could persuade her into making the same mistake as her mother, he was way off line. Never, never, never would she become a rich man's mistress, no matter how powerful the attraction. And she hated him for evoking such a wanton weakness in her.

'You won!' she said bitterly. 'And now it is finished. Please go!'

'If this is winning, then I've lost,' he murmured cryptically, passionately.

He swung her around to face him and Bernadette still hadn't recovered enough to resist his strength. Her eyes flared at him with all the fury of wounded pride.

'Take your hands off me, Danton Fayette. Now and forever! Or I'll scream this place down. And you'll regret that until the day you die.'

They were wild, hysterical words, but she didn't care, as long as he knew how passionately she rejected him and any power he thought he had over her.

His face hardened momentarily, then the taunting mockery leapt back into the compelling black eyes. 'Certainly,' he said, and the mockery was back in his voice as well. His head tilted back. His eyes narrowed into piercing darts that struck straight at her soul. 'If that *is* what you want.'

The shared knowledge of what she had wanted a few minutes ago writhed through her, whipping Bernadette into a frenzy of shame. 'It's precisely what I want!' she bit out, fiercely denying that terrible, mindless desire.

He picked his hands off her shoulders and smiled, a slow, lazy smile that had little humour in it. 'So we cannot play it straight,' he drawled. 'And I will have to do it my way. Your obduracy leaves me no choice. You will have to be taught.'

Taught what? Bernadette thought in furious outrage at his arrogance. It was he who had to be taught he couldn't have every woman he fancied. At least she was one who would not fall victim to the temporary excitement he offered.

He sauntered over to the balustrade, turned, leaned his back against it and folded his arms. 'Your father wants to buy my island from me,' he stated with lazy uninterest. 'Did he tell you that?'

'Yes,' Bernadette snapped, impatient with herself for still staying with him when the sensible thing was to walk away.

'It's one of the few natural paradises left on this earth,' he said softly. 'Still unspoiled by modern civilisation. Life there is a simple, happy affair. Not ruled by the clock. No stress. No strain. The native Polynesians are almost all pure-bred. A remarkable people, really. Open and friendly. I think you would like them.'

He paused. Bernadette felt bewildered by the change of topic, and piqued that he could switch from passionate desire to a casual exposition of his island's attractions in the space of a minute or two.

'Of course, that situation is unlikely to last if your father builds a huge modern holiday resort there,' Danton continued, as if musing over the problem. 'On the other hand, one must consider that he has offered me an enormous sum for it.'

'Do you need the money, Danton?' Bernadette shot at him sarcastically.

'No. As a matter of fact I have wealth enough to last me several lifetimes.' He smiled at her like a shark who had fed well.

And that was what he was! A sleek, devouring shark! Bernadette turned to go, disgusted with herself for being the least bit attracted to him.

'Wait!' he said imperiously.

Why she didn't ignore him, Bernadette didn't know, but her feet stopped moving and her heart leapt in treacherous anticipation.

'Please turn around,' he said in a low, persuasive tone that spun an even more effective web around her, holding her.

She struggled against his magnetism. 'Why?' she demanded, needing it to be ended yet unable to pull away.

'Because I want to watch your face.'

'No.' At least she could drag up that much independence.

'I have a proposition for you.'

Her back stiffened. 'I'm not interested.'

'A business proposition.'

Her curiosity was piqued enough to hear what he had to say. Bernadette concentrated hard on presenting a face that projected nothing more than the coldest interest. Then she turned, very slowly, stiff with the most impenetrable dignity.

Danton hadn't moved. His face was set in a casually ruthless expression, his eyes oddly opaque.

No devilish amusement, no mockery, no dangerous glitter . . . just an intense watchfulness that revealed nothing of what he was thinking.

'A business proposition?' she said with mocking disbelief.

His mouth curled ever so slightly. 'As you know, your father wants to buy my island. I'm going to let you decide whether or not I sell it to him.'

'Then I decide in my father's favour!' she snapped, not pausing to think, reacting against Danton rather than for her father.

'Is that how you make a fair judgement, Bernadette?' he asked, a bleak look crossing his face before his mouth firmed into grim ruthlessness. 'There is one condition before your decision is final.'

And suddenly the dangerous glitter was back in his eyes. Bernadette tensed, every instinct on the alert against attack.

'For one month . . . you must come and live on the island. When the month is up, whatever decision you make . . . whether Te Enata is to pass into your father's hands or not . . . that decision will be binding and irrevocable. One month of your time, Bernadette, to decide the islanders' future. That is the proposition!'

CHAPTER SIX

BERNADETTE had never heard a more unbusinesslike proposition. It made no sense to her . . . yet it was inescapable that Danton was trying to manipulate her, or the situation, either for himself or for the people who lived on Te Enata.

'This is absurd, what you're doing,' she tossed at him, hoping to goad him into a more forthright explanation of his motives.

'Perhaps.' His manner was languid . . . assured . . . unprickable.

'Why are you making this ridiculous proposal?' she demanded, needing some show of cards.

'It serves my purpose.'

Something in the way he looked at her . . . was it an acquisitive gleam? Would he go that far—gamble the future of his island—simply for the chance of getting what he wanted from her? It seemed so extreme—reckless and obsessive.

Bernadette tried to quell her inner agitation, but her body didn't seem to obey her commands when she was around Danton Fayette. He couldn't want her that much . . . could he? Had no other woman challenged him? Rejected him? Her mind sought to test the disturbing idea that satisfying his desire for her meant more to him than anything else . . . that he didn't care what else happened, as long as he could have her.

'No doubt you intend to be on the island for the same month I am there?' she tossed at him with dry mockery.

'Certainly,' he replied, completely unabashed. He smiled that slow, lazy smile that slid under her skin and made her prickle. 'I wouldn't want you to miss anything, Bernadette. I intend to give you every assistance in coming to your decision.'

'Taking time out to seduce me at your leisure,' she sliced back at him. 'Or so you think.'

'Only a woman who wants to be seduced surrenders, Bernadette,' he said silkily. 'Of course, if you can't trust yourself with me . . . if you don't think you can keep to your . . . principles . . . for a month—one short month—then by all means refuse.'

He was tempting her with another contest.

'You expect me to live with you?' Bernadette asked, probing for the full picture.

'Do you want to?' he countered, one eyebrow rising in quizzical expectation.

'No,' she answered unequivocally.

'Then you shall have a separate residence.'

But he would get to her. Bernadette did not delude herself about that. He would get to her in any way he could. And she was vulnerable to him. She might like to prove that her principles could stick against his powerful attraction, but he was out to win and she was not at all sure she would not

lose to him . . . some time. And then what? The
stakes were much higher now. It would cost her
more than a loss of pride. It might cost her body
and soul!

'No. I won't go,' she said decisively.

He shrugged. 'What a pity!' He unfolded his
arms and straightened up as if the matter no longer
concerned him. 'That's what your father said you
would say,' he tossed at her carelessly. 'I hope you
didn't mind my asking, in spite of what he said.'

'My father?' Bernadette's voice gathered a shrill
edge as a host of implications swarmed into her
mind. 'You put this proposition to my father?'

'Yes. This afternoon,' he answered, as if the
point was now irrelevant. He turned and picked up
his wig and mask, already wiping his hands of the
whole affair. Which just went to prove how little
he had cared about her! All he had wanted was to
entertain himself with another conquest!

As for her father, Bernadette was livid with rage
that he had even discussed such a proposition with
Danton Fayette. He didn't need the island. It was
merely an extension of his gigantic ego to own one.
Part of his *grand design*!

It was something towards his credit that he had
at least known that she would say no, but
Bernadette had no doubt that he would have
pushed Alicia or Alex to do his bidding. Pawns in
the game! Bought by his wealth and locked into his
hip-pocket! Thank goodness she had had the sense
not to have fallen into that trap!

Danton picked up her mask and handed it to

her. 'Shall we return to the ballroom?' The black
eyes glinted with devilry as he added. 'I'm sure
your father is getting anxious about our long
absence.'

'Waiting for confirmation of my answer, you
mean,' she retorted bitterly.

He moved his lips in teasing consideration. 'Who
knows? It should be interesting to see his reaction.'

'Yes,' she hissed in seething resentment.

He gave that soft little laugh that raised her
hackles and moved on to the door, opening it for
her and waving her forward with a foppishly
elegant half-bow, mockingly resuming his Louis
the Fourteenth character although he didn't bother
replacing his wig and mask.

Bernadette didn't bother with her mask either.
Although it was not yet midnight, the ball was over
as far as she was concerned. She swept past
Danton, head held high, and sailed straight for the
stairs, not waiting for him to accompany her.

She gritted her teeth as she saw her father
standing at the foot of the staircase, the harem girl
still in close attendance. What was he waiting for:
to see if Danton had won the contest or to gauge if
there was any chance that she might help him get
the island he wanted?

There was only one result of this evening's
business that concerned Bernadette. She was never
going to have anything more to do with her father
or Danton Fayette again!

She had barely begun her descent when Gerard
Hamilton darted a worried glance upwards. He

had discarded his mask and the white sheikh head-dress seemed to rob his face of colour. It looked grey and strained. His gaze lingered momentarily on Bernadette's cold expression, then stabbed over her shoulder. Bernadette was well aware that Danton was only a step or two behind her, but she disdained to acknowledge his presence. She was finished with Danton Fayette.

Her father's expression suddenly changed to one of grim determination. He took to the stairs, reaching the central landing as Bernadette stepped on to it. His eyes raked her stony face, then moved sharply to Danton who remained one step up, assuming a subtle dominance in the meeting.

'You put it to her . . . about the island. Didn't you? Even though I told you not to,' Gerard grated in angry accusation.

Danton smiled. 'Of course. The choice was hers as much as yours, Gerard,' he said, totally unruffled by the fury emanating from his host.

Gerard swung back to Bernadette, eyes blazing with impassioned feeling. 'I don't want you to go, Bernadette. I turned down Danton's proposition this afternoon. He can keep his damned island forever! You are far more important to me.'

He grasped her hand in his anxiety to impress his sincerity on her. 'I swear to you I'm telling you the truth. Believe me, Bernadette, I have no part in this. None whatsoever!'

Bernadette turned to Danton. He wore a cynical smile and the black eyes danced with devilry. She believed her father. And she fiercely resented

Danton's malicious amusement. He had deliberately led her to think her father was an interested party to his proposition. He had wanted to hurt . . . a malevolent revenge for her rejection of him.

And he was enjoying her father's distress!

If only she could make him pay! Humble him as he had humbled her tonight!

He had stripped her of her pride, made a fool of her father, deceived him into thinking that the island was for sale, while all the time the proposition had only been a manipulative game.

And Danton was still laughing behind that taunting little smile.

Bernadette's wounded pride swelled into fierce resolution. She was not going to let him get away with beating them, and there was only one way to even the score. She had to change her mind and accept Danton's proposition. It was now a matter of honour!

Her chin tilted. Her eyes burnt with fiery purpose as she delivered her challenge. 'I finish my present job at the end of next week. I will come to Te Enata then, for the full month . . .'

'No!' Gerard cut in. 'Don't do it, Bernadette. You don't know him as I do.'

'I will, Father,' she said curtly, her eyes never leaving Danton's. 'Whatever decision I make about the sale of the island will be binding and irrevocable,' she continued, mocking him with his own words. 'Don't forget that, Danton. I want to see that agreement legally drawn up and signed by you before I leave Sydney.'

'It will be done,' he said.

Bernadette offered a smile of her own—one cased in icy promise. 'And I swear to you now . . . whatever the decision is that you want, Danton . . . you will not get it even if you beg for it.'

'Bernadette, for pity's sake, listen to me!' Gerard burst out in desperation.

Bernadette wrenched her gaze from Danton's and looked hard at her father, seeing the anguished concern in his eyes and realising for the first time that he did care for her. It wasn't simply pride. He cared!

She squeezed his hand in a warm rush of feeling. 'Don't worry about me. I know what I'm doing.'

He shook his head. 'No. You do not.'

Impossible to change her mind now. He knew Bernadette too well not to recognise her resolution. He swung to the man who had ruthlessly manipulated this situation beyond Gerard's power to stop it, and all the steel that had gone into accumulating wealth and power slid into his voice.

'Damn you, Danton Fayette! Hurt my daughter . . . through me . . . and you'll have to watch your back for the rest of your life.'

'Gerard . . .' Danton shook his head in reproach. 'You mustn't excite yourself. It's so dangerous,' he said softly. 'Trust me. I will take the greatest care of your daughter. I understand why you are jealous of her. After all, she is a pearl beyond price, is she not?' His mouth twitched with mocking humour. 'Do you really think I would undervalue such a prize?'

Then he smiled at Bernadette, the black eyes gleaming with anticipation. 'I look forward to welcoming you to Te Enata. Until next week, Bernadette.'

He gave them a jaunty salute and left them, a lithe spring in his step as he made his way towards the reception foyer.

Bernadette turned to her father whose gaze had also followed Danton. 'I owe you an apology,' she said softly.

He sighed and turned a tired, strained face to her. 'I wish . . .' A bleak pride stiffened his expression. 'Perhaps one day you will listen to me . . . with an open mind.'

He didn't wait for an answer. He turned, stepped over to the banister and clutched it hard, then slowly, wearily he began mounting the left-hand branch of the staircase.

'Gerard?' It was the harem girl, her masked face lifted to him, her voice high and anxious.

He paused for a moment and looked down at her. 'I'm all right, Tammy. I'll be down again soon. Wait for me here.'

Bernadette watched him trudge up the stairs, alarm streaking through her mind: his grey face . . . Danton warning it was dangerous to get excited . . . Jeffrey, who drove her father everywhere, suggesting she make her peace with her father before anything happened.

It was his heart!

Angina pectoris . . . arteriosclerosis . . . the possibilities came racing out of her medical experience.

And he might need attention right now!

Did he have Anginine tablets?

Bernadette started up the stairs after him but the harem-girl caught her arm. 'No. You mustn't go. He doesn't want you to, Bernadette,' she pleaded in an urgent whisper.

'I'm a doctor,' Bernadette stated curtly, impatient at being held back when her father might need help.

'His own specialist is here. The valet will call him if it's necessary,' came the quick retort. 'Please, Bernadette! He doesn't like anyone to see him when he's like this. Not even me. You have to believe me!'

She wrung her hands, distressed with her role of supplicant but driven to take this stand for Gerard's sake. 'Please, don't upset him further. I'm not putting this very well. Whether you despise me for what I am or not . . . you must believe that I . . . I love your father. I'd do anything for him. And you . . . you don't know what you do, Bernadette. I don't want him hurt . . .'

Bernadette stared incredulously at the woman . . . the woman who now performed the services once supplied by Bernadette's mother. Revulsion swept through her, and bitterness leapt off her tongue. 'What do you know about hurt?'

There was an instant drawing up of dignity: head tilting back, shoulders squared. 'You're not the

only one who has had to suffer from the past,'
she said slowly, decisively. 'I would do anything
to bring you and your father closer together. And
you must appreciate that whatever happened, it
was nothing to do with me. It was not my
fault.'

'You think it's my fault?' Bernadette retorted
fiercely.

The woman stood her ground without so much
as a flinch. 'I don't know. All I know is he
hurts . . . over you. And he's a proud man. He'd
never let you see how he hurts.'

Proud . . . yes, Bernadette understood that very
well. She wouldn't show him what she felt, either.
Nor would she have ever told him if she were ill.
And maybe that was wrong. He did care about her.
He had proved that tonight. He didn't want her to
be hurt. And despite all that had happened in the
past . . . he was her father.

'You're sure he is being well cared for?'
Bernadette asked.

'Yes!' came the prompt answer. 'He has the best
specialist there is. And I look after him as much as
he allows me. I am a trained nurse.'

'It is his heart?' Bernadette needed to know that
her diagnosis was correct.

'Yes. There's arethema in the coronary wall and
they're considering him for a bypass operation.'

'Who is his specialist?'

'Dr Norton.'

He was the best heart specialist Bernadette knew.
She had heard him lecture and seen him at work in

surgery. Her father was in good hands. And, having weighed all the information she had received, Bernadette relaxed. There was no need to follow him. She turned her full attention on to the harem girl.

'Thank you for telling me. I won't let on that I know.'

'Thank you,' the woman sighed, and wearily lifted off her mask.

Bernadette felt a ripple of shock as she realised that Tammy Gardner was only a few years older than herself—possibly thirty but certainly no more than that. Her face was lovely. Fresh-looking. Not like the hardened model Bernadette had imagined.

The woman gave an ironic smile. 'You think I'm too young to love him. But I do.'

Bernadette raised cynical eyes. She had heard words like that before—protestations of pure love untainted by greed—and found them false too many times to ever give them much credit. She found it easier to deal with people when their motives were out in the open.

'It's not the money?' she asked softly.

The smile was instantly cut off and angry pride blazed back at her. 'If I ever have to leave your father, I will go away with precisely what I came with. No one will ever be able to throw that accusation at me.'

Bernadette reassessed the woman, believed what she saw, slowly relaxed. 'I'm sorry. I shouldn't have said that. Please don't be offended. It's something that . . . that haunts me,' she said in painful excuse. Her eyes searched for understanding. 'Doesn't it bother you that there's been a line of others before you?' she asked, miserably conscious that her mother had been one of them.

'What does it matter? He's mine now.'

Bernadette shook her head, unable to accept that attitude. She tried for enlightenment. 'He . . . doesn't want to marry you?'

'Why would we spoil what we've got? Your father is very fond of me. And as long as he wants me with him, I'll stay. If it's only for a few years, they will be years I will treasure for the rest of my life.'

The earnest conviction with which she said the words shook Bernadette's preconceptions. There were layers of life here she didn't understand. Her mind groped for a clearer perception, trying to look at things from angles she had never explored before.

Had her mother felt like Tammy?

Could she herself ever feel like that about a man?

And Danton slid through her mind . . . ever tantalising . . . driving her into a passion that wiped out everything else.

She shivered.

Tammy placed a tentative hand on Bernadette's arm, and there was a knowledge in her beautiful green eyes that belied her relatively young age. 'Your father is an honest man, Bernadette. Not

perfect. No one of his brilliance ever is. They're
different from ordinary people . . . like me. He's
made mistakes he deeply regrets. And he's paid
dearly for them. More dearly than ordinary people.
It's only those who climb high hills that have a long
way to fall. But if you do ever come to
him—please, I beg you—let it be to meet him half-
way.'

To listen with an open mind . . .

Bernadette rubbed at her forehead, trying to
clear the buzz of thoughts.

Danton telling her that she had been obsessed
with herself . . . her mind narrowed by
circumstance . . . black and white.

Had she been wrong? Wrong about her
father . . . wrong about other things? What was
happening didn't seem to be making much sense.
Patterns of behaviour simply weren't clicking
together in a way she could recognise . . . or
identify with.

'Bernadette? Are you all right?'

'Yes. I'm tired. I think it's time I went home.'
She managed an apologetic smile. 'I'm sorry if I
offended you. Thanks for talking to me, Tammy.'

An embarrassed pleasure suffused the lovely
face. 'I'm glad you're not offended.'

'Not at all. I'm pleased to have met you,'
Bernadette said automatically, then realised it was
the truth. She squeezed the other woman's hand
and smiled. 'Maybe we shall meet again. Who
knows? Thank you again. And goodnight. Thank
you for everything.'

She spotted Alex signalling a waiter for more drinks and made her way over to him, determined not to be found wanting in manners, even though he probably didn't care a fig what she did.

He caught sight of her and strolled to meet her, his mouth curling into a sardonic twist. 'Very bad form, unmasking before midnight, dear sis. I can see you need some tuition at these things. Wouldn't want you disgracing the family. You can call on me at any time for expert advice.'

'Thank you, Alex. I'm not staying any longer. I wanted to say goodnight,' Bernadette said briskly.

He shrugged. '*C'est la vie!* But one small word in your ear. Danton Fayette is a most untrustworthy chap. He suggested this damned costume and then turned up in it himself. And a better one than mine. Very bad form!'

'It seems we're both guilty of bad form,' she commented ironically. 'Goodnight, Alex.'

Bernadette found Alicia near the entrance to the ballroom and took leave of her also.

'I'll see you out and have the car called for you,' Alicia said graciously. Then, as they drew away from the other guests, she whispered anxiously, 'Is anything wrong? Father won't be pleased if . . .'

'No, nothing's wrong,' Bernadette assured her drily. Except that black and white had slipped into so many shades that they needed a lot of intensive examination.

It was a relief to sink on to the back seat of the

Rolls and have Jeffrey drive her away.

'You're leaving early, Miss Bernadette,' the chauffeur observed, his eyes scanning her inquisitively in the rear-vision mirror.

'Not really,' she said wearily. 'I feel as if my whole life has passed before me. Just take me home please, Jeffrey. I don't want to talk. There are a great many things I've got to sort out.'

Like her life!

He drove the rest of the way in silence, then accompanied her up to her apartment floor. Once her door was unlocked, he tipped his cap and offered her a sympathetic smile. 'Goodnight, Miss Bernadette. I'm sorry the night didn't work out well for you.'

She sighed and smiled back. 'Maybe it did, Jeffrey. Time will tell. Goodnight. And thank you.'

She went inside and closed the door, but she was all too aware that a lot of other doors had opened tonight . . . doors that she couldn't close, that necessitated a reassessment of everything she had ever thought.

About her aims . . .

About her principles . . .

About her father . . .

And Danton . . . Danton, playing his subtle sleight-of-hand games . . . a catalyst who exploded everything that had gone before, and reshaped her neatly drawn world into something different.

CHAPTER SEVEN

DANTON FAYETTE left nothing to chance.

The morning after New Year's Day, a man from the French Embassy called at Bernadette's apartment with the papers for a visa and a request for her passport so that the papers could be processed. That same evening her airline ticket was delivered—a first-class flight to Papeete on January the tenth. She would be met there and flown by private charter to Te Enata.

Attached to the papers was a handwritten note from Danton: 'There is no doctor on the island. Bring your medical bag if you like to be useful.'

It was a provocative touch, typical of him. She remembered telling him six years ago, with all the scorn of her youthful idealism, that he led a totally useless life. Had she wounded his pride then? Was he intent on proving another point now?

Bernadette fought against the feeling that a trap was closing around her. She assured herself that Danton Fayette was not the kind of man who would ever resort to force. Manipulation, yes, but never force.

She knew him better now, knew what he was capable of. Surely she could defend herself against his clever manoeuvres? Being with Danton for a month was simply something she had to get through. Like a term at boarding-school . . . or a tough set of examinations. It kept her apprehension at bay to think of it like that, but sometimes her stomach clenched with tension in spite of her reasoning.

She completed her locum work and spent a couple of hectic days shopping. For a month on a tropical island she needed a range of casual clothes that she didn't normally wear.

Her father telephoned to offer assistance in making travel arrangements, but Bernadette told him the only assistance she required was a lift to Mascot Airport on the morning of departure. In truth, she was simply using that request in order to see him without being too obvious about it. She wanted to check that he was all right . . . and speak to him face to face.

The habits of a lifetime did not shift easily. Bernadette could not bring herself to ask for a direct meeting with no other purpose but to talk to him. Even when he came and accompanied her to Mascot, she could not change the conversational pattern they had used for so many years . . . a thrust and parry of words that revealed nothing of what they felt.

But he looked well. Fighting fit. No one would ever guess he had a heart problem. His face had good colour, his eyes held a lively sparkle, and all his movements held the spring of good health. She hoped nothing would happen to him while she was away.

Jeffrey took in her bags at the airport and wished her a happy holiday.

Her father helped her through the official checking in.

They sat in the Captain's Club Lounge, waiting for the flight to Tahiti to be called. Nothing of any moment had been said. Bernadette desperately wanted to ask him about her mother, to ask why he had done what he had done, but pride still held her tongue.

Instead she asked about Danton Fayette, needing some release from her inner tension.

'Tell me all you know about him,' she invited, hoping that a knowledge of his background might be helpful in the battle ahead of her. And battle it would be . . . Bernadette had no delusions about that. She had to fight the weakness in herself as well as defend against Danton's strengths.

Gerard Hamilton nodded approval. He always investigated the backgrounds of people he dealt with. He relaxed back in his armchair and related what he knew.

'The Fayettes are a family of merchant bankers that had connections with the Paris Rothschilds. Danton studied law but never practised it. He rose to prominence as an international money-fund manager at quite an early age. The good ones usually do. He would only be in his mid-thirties now.'

Perhaps a decade between them, Bernadette thought. Years of experience that she couldn't

match, but she would make up for it in will-power.
She had to. Or she would end up like her
mother . . . giving in to a man like her father. And
she couldn't let that happen.

Her father continued with barely a pause. 'When
you first met him, Danton was setting up shelf
companies for trust operations throughout the
Pacific region: Tahiti, Nouméa, Vanuatu, Brunei.
In these latter years he has not been so active on the
scene. He has managers in Switzerland, Hol-
land . . .' His gesture encompassed more of the
same kind of thing. 'Danton Fayette has always
been one step ahead of the game, Bernadette.
Don't underestimate him.'

'I won't,' she said with more confidence than she
felt. If only she didn't find him so attractive . . .
'Has he ever been married?'

'No. He plays fast and loose. I doubt there's
been any woman who's held his interest for long.'
His gaze rested thoughtfully on Bernadette, and he
wondered . . .

'What about the island?' she asked. 'You must
have visited it.'

He nodded. 'Danton invited me there three years
ago. Looking back on it, that's when he started to
set this operation up, get me interested. Te Enata is
very beautiful. Idyllic. Apart from the plantation
homestead, it's still rather primitive. Not much
more than a general store on one side of it, and a
small village on the other. And the huts of the
islanders. Supplies are brought in by boat.'

'The plantation?' she prompted.

'It's not an economic proposition any more. Danton doesn't even try to run it as a business. It's just an upkeep operation that pays wages.'

'How did he come to own the island in the first place?' Bernadette rattled on, more to keep talking than out of any real curiosity. None of this mattered. What was going to happen between her and Danton was all that mattered. She had been a fool to accept the challenge. It was madness to put herself in such jeopardy, and yet . . . she wanted . . . no, she had to go now. It *was* a matter of honour!

'The island came to him from his grandfather—on his mother's side,' her father explained. 'He bought it before the First World War. Set up the plantation—copra, sugar, pineapples . . . they made a lot of money in their time.'

He frowned. 'But that's beside the point. It surprised me when I heard the island was on the market . . . for the right price. If I owned it, I would never sell. Not under any circumstances.'

'He doesn't want to sell it,' Bernadette said with certainty. 'Danton always does the opposite of what you would expect. He's gambling that I'll give in to him.'

Their eyes met, their mutual understanding sharp and complete. That strange semblance of a smile crossed Gerard's mouth. 'Maybe I was wrong. You might be a match for him, Bernadette. One way or another . . .'

Bernadette forced a smile. 'I'm glad you have some faith in me. What kind of resort do you intend building, Father?'

It took him a few moments to re-concentrate his mind. 'There would have to be a central complex, of course. Reception, restaurants, entertainment areas, staff quarters. But the guest accommodation would be individual cabins. With a whole island, one doesn't have to scrimp on space, and I would want to retain the natural charm of the place. Tennis courts and a golf course would have to be fitted in. A must for the type of people I want to attract. They'd love it.'

Bernadette nodded, uneasy in her own mind over what might happen to the present way of life on Te Enata. Danton's argument did have substance. She had been to Hawaii and knew there was nothing left of the original culture except an ersatz display for tourists. But maybe the intrusion of Western society from her father's holiday resort could be strictly limited. She could insist on it. Her father would owe her that concession.

The flight was called.

They stood up.

Her father accompanied Bernadette to the departure gate and she was conscious of every step they took, heart-thumpingly aware that time was running out on her and she hadn't spoken any part of what she had meant to say to him. There were so many things she ached to know. And she did care about him. But how to say it? How to reach out to him?

She lingered with him while the boarding-line of passengers went through the gate, still hopelessly tongue-tied. The last passenger was processed and the airline stewardess looked enquiringly at Bernadette.

She turned stiffly to her father and held out her hand. 'Goodbye. Thank you for seeing me off.'

His hand gripped hers warmly. 'Take care, Bernadette.'

'You, too,' she said huskily, her throat suddenly thick with a welling lump of emotion.

She drew her hand away, half turned, and the regret ploughing through her heart was so sharp that she couldn't leave . . . not with nothing said. She swung back, a self-conscious rush of colour sweeping into her cheeks.

'Meet me when I come back?'

'I will,' he assured her. And there was something in his eyes . . . something warmer than pride.

There was no time to say more, but, driven to make some meaningful gesture, she stepped closer to him, reached up and pressed a kiss to his cheek.

She didn't look back as she went through the gate. She didn't look back at all. Gerard watched her until she had disappeared into the tunnel that would take her to the plane. His eyes blurred with tears, but he didn't care if anyone saw them.

The ice of twelve years was melting. Nothing was more important than that.

He touched his cheek where she had kissed him.

And in a month's time he would be here to meet

her . . . to welcome his daughter home. Be damned if he was going to die on Norton's operating table when he had so much to live for! Besides, his heart felt great! He felt better than he had for a long, long time.

And Bernadette felt better too. She relaxed into the wide first-class passenger seat and accepted a glass of champagne from the stewardess. She felt more at peace with herself than she had all week, more than she had in years. And when she came home she would open up to her father . . . meet him half-way, as Tammy Gardner had said.

Meanwhile, she had to get her mind focused on the immediate problem . . . Danton . . . and a month with him on Te Enata. How was she going to block his attraction? She couldn't let him win. Not this time. She had to show him that, no matter what he did, she could stick to her principles!

The six-and-a-half-hour flight to Tahiti passed all too quickly. Bernadette had still not formed any concrete plan of action—or defence—when the jet set down at Faaa Airport. She was met at the customs line by a man who introduced himself as Alain Perdrier, her transport officer to Te Enata.

It was mid-morning and the tropical heat and humidity hit her like a wave as they left the international airport. Bernadette wished she had thought to ask her father more about the plantation homestead. She hoped it was air-conditioned. She also hoped her clothes didn't wilt on her before she arrived at Te Enata.

For this initial confrontation with Danton she had chosen to wear a very fashionable white trouser-suit in a polyester-linen. The coat was a long shirt-style with loose three-quarter-length sleeves, smartly cuffed. She had teamed it with a sleeveless yellow T-shirt, and yellow and white strappy sandals.

The outfit was complemented by a soft white linen sunhat, an eye-catching yellow scarf wrapped spectacularly around its crown. Bernadette had rolled her long blonde hair into a coil at the nape of her neck so she could position the hat at a slightly jaunty angle. She wanted to look like a woman who had everything together. Unassailable . . . in every sense!

However, her plan for a dignified arrival was somewhat undermined when she discovered that her chartered flight was on a sea-plane. She was faced with the prospect of getting into and out of a runabout dinghy in order to board and leave the small flying-craft. Alain Perdrier explained there was no airstrip at Te Enata. One either travelled by boat or sea-plane, but flying the distance was better. It only took an hour.

Bernadette resigned herself to the inevitable. She stepped into the rocky boat, intensely grateful that her sandals did not have high heels. She hung grimly on to her hat while they chugged across the water to the sea-plane. No matter how unsettling this last leg of the trip was, she was determined to rise above everything and show Danton an imperturbable face!

Forty-five minutes later the island came into view, and as they flew closer it looked like a fabulous jewel in the sea.

It was surrounded by a rim of white surf crashing against the coral reef. Within that outer perimeter, the lagoon waters were a luminous opal green, shading into light turquoise against the bleached coral grit of the beaches. The vegetation was a brilliant green, so thick it looked like rainforest, except for the waving palm-trees around the shore.

Bernadette could see no sign of habitation at all, apart from a few large huts clustered at the land end of a long pier.

As the sea-plane zoomed down to a landing on the lagoon, figures ran out to the beach and launched canoes into the water. Bernadette hoped she wasn't expected to get into one of them in order to reach dry land again. The plane skimmed towards the pier and finally came to a halt quite close to it. One of the natives rowed a dinghy over to the passenger door and Bernadette eyed it with relief. At least it was better than a canoe!

By the time she had lowered herself into it, the canoes were all around her, the natives tossing leis into the boat and calling out 'Bienvenue' or 'Haere mai' which Bernadette took to be the Polynesian welcome. She saw, with something of a shock, that underneath their leis the girls were bare-breasted. All of them! And the men wore a distracting amount of tattoos on their arms and chests.

After a few mind-stunned moments, Bernadette lifted two of the frangipani leis over her head. Their colour didn't clash with her clothes and she didn't wish to give offence. The rest she hung over her wrist. Everyone smiled and seemed happy with that.

When she glanced up at the pier, Danton was there, waiting for her. He had appeared from nowhere. But not the sleek, sophisticated man she was familiar with.

He wore nothing but a short native pareu slung around his hips, vividly patterned in red and white. It showed off the dark tan of his all too naked body; a body that was emphatically male and stunningly beautiful.

Bernadette had never applied the word 'beautiful' to a man before, but it slid into her mind and stuck. Every line and contour was in perfect proportion; his flesh was firm, his skin smooth and gleaming. The lithe animal grace when he moved kept her eyes fastened on him . . . fascinated . . . mesmerised!

Bernadette suddenly remembered his argument of six years ago—his preoccupation with the sensual—but he had been wrong then and he was wrong now. He was not going to make the ground rules for the next thirty days. And no way was she going to go 'native'.

The dinghy bumped beside a ladder at the end of the pier. Danton bent down a hand to help Bernadette up the couple of steps. The moment he grasped her wrist, Bernadette's pulse started racing. Fight as they would . . . as they must . . . he was the only man who had ever excited such a reaction from her.

It wasn't until she was firmly balanced on the pier and she met the amused twinkle in those devilish black eyes that she started to recollect herself.

'So . . . you came,' he murmured, his gaze skating down her outfit and back up to her hat, while a smile slowly spread across his face. 'Even if it is only to do battle,' he added mockingly.

Bernadette waited until his eyes met hers again, and smiled her disdain of him and all he stood for. 'You cannot expect me to like you, Danton. And neither you nor your ideas are important to me. The only reason I'm here is because it pleases me to do something for my father.'

The lines of his face fractionally tightened. 'I will not argue with you when I'm your host.'

She raised her eyebrow in sceptical question. 'You don't intend to try to change my mind?'

'About many things.' His mouth curled. 'But not by arguing. Come . . .' He took a light hold on her arm to start her walking with him down the pier, and swept out his other arm to encompass their surroundings. 'Te Enata will be a wonderful experience for you. There are two places I know of in the whole world which are wonderful for healing . . . where the wounded get better. Switzerland is one . . .' His eyes slid provocatively to hers. 'The islands of Tahiti is the other.'

'Are you implying that I'm wounded, Danton?' she said with dry mockery. 'That there is something wrong with me?'

'Which of us is perfect?' he replied enigmatically. 'Look around you, Bernadette. The inhibitions and neuroses generated by our sophisticated Western society do not touch these people. The men and women are at ease with their bodies, happy with the simplicity of their lives . . .' He looked directly at her. 'Can you say the same thing?'

He was deliberately trying to confuse her. Bernadette shook her head. 'I have no phobias,' she said dismissively.

A little boy came pelting down the pier, and Danton released Bernadette's arm to catch him and lift him up high before lowering the delighted child to his shoulder.

'The most important thing here . . .' he said, the black eyes holding hers intently '. . . is children. They are valued above all else. They are not personal possessions to be neglected or cherished at one person's whim. They are a gift from God to be loved by everyone.'

'How convenient!' Bernadette snapped, an angry flush rising to her cheeks at Danton's pointed reference to her own background. 'Are you the father of this boy who can be left so happily to others?'

'Yes. In a way,' he said, completely unabashed. He set the boy down and the child promptly leapt off the pier to join a group of others splashing in the water.

Danton returned his gaze to Bernadette. 'I'm a father to all of them. But not in the sense you mean,' he said quietly. 'When I father children, it will be with the woman I want above all others. And my wife and children will be together . . . in the ways that really count . . . for the rest of our lives.'

Bernadette had no ready answer for that. Again he had confused all her preconceptions of him. Was he really capable of constancy? Fidelity? Or was this a feint . . . a sleight-of-hand gambit in his game to seduce her?

'I'll believe that when I see it happen, Danton,' she said. 'Particularly after I meet your wife.'

The taunting twinkle came back to his eyes. 'I wonder what kind of mother you would make, Bernadette.'

'It's not likely that I'll ever get married,' she said curtly.

'No, of course not,' he mocked. 'That would mean having to face the fact that you're a woman.'

Bernadette clamped her lips together, refusing to rise to his bait. A typical male chauvinist, she thought savagely, and she was not about to be drawn into a stupid sexist discussion.

'But Te Enata will work its magic on you. Here you will know you are a woman. Above all else,' he said, deliberately taking her silence to mean agreement with him. 'Nothing is more sure. Nothing more certain.'

And with that promise . . . or threat . . . he led

her off the pier and on to his island.

The idea of Danton Fayette being a benevolent philanthropist, caring about her welfare, bringing her to his island for a month so that her 'wounds' might be healed, was too much for Bernadette to swallow. Besides, she knew how devious he was. Sooner or later he would show his real hand, and she had to keep her mind clear to recognise it when it came. And deal with it!

'I'll take you to your hut so you can settle in before lunch,' he said as he steered her towards a jeep.

'Hut?' Bernadette gritted his teeth. 'You own a house here, Danton,' she said with pointed emphasis.

'But you said you wanted a separate residence. So separate we are.' His eyes glittered with unholy amusement. 'See how fair I am? I keep to my word.'

So much for her welfare! she thought furiously. But she could not argue with him, and she would not beg! She had laid down that condition and, however primitive the hut was, she would live in it even if it killed her. Only a month, she told her sinking heart.

Out in the sun the heat was sweltering, and she gladly accepted Danton's hand up into the jeep. At least it had a canvas roof to provide some shade. Her clothes were already sticking to her from the humidity. The sooner she could change into something cooler, the better. There certainly wasn't going to be any air-conditioning in a hut!

'What about my luggage?' she asked as Danton climbed into the driver's seat. A glance down the pier showed it was still being unloaded from the dinghy.

'It will be brought to you soon enough,' he answered.

'I prefer to wait for it now,' Bernadette said determinedly. A hut was bad enough. She was not going to sit around in these hot clothes for hours, waiting for her luggage to be delivered.

Danton shrugged. 'As you wish.'

The engine of the sea-plane started up and the little craft began to manoeuvre into position for take-off. Bernadette watched it skim down the lagoon and lift into the air. As it climbed away, she felt a sharp sense of being cut off from the world she knew.

And then Danton spelled it out!

'You now have no way off the island, Bernadette,' he said, drawing her gaze back to him. The black eyes gleamed with intense satisfaction. 'Whatever happens! There is nowhere to run. No one to scream for. Your father can't save you here. For the next month you are mine!'

CHAPTER EIGHT

SO . . . at last he had revealed his true colours. No subtlety! No hidden cards! If this was Danton Fayette's idea of a grand coup, he had a lot to learn. Certainly about her! And Bernadette was more than ready to start teaching him. The sheer blazing arrogance of the man had her spitting fire.

'Don't think I'm some kind of prisoner, Danton!' she threw at him scathingly. 'And don't think you can do what you want with me. Remember I hold the fate of this island in my hands. So I'll set you straight on a few ground rules . . .'

'What a good idea!'

His amusement added fuel to the flame. '. . . for your behaviour while I'm staying here!' Bernadette hissed.

He smiled invitingly. 'Please go ahead.'

She drew in a deep breath to cool her brain. 'One. You will not limit my freedom of movement in any way. For whatever reason you engineered this situation, the proposition stands as far as I'm concerned, and I'll go wherever I like and do whatever I like on this island.'

'Certainly. Once I see you settled in your hut, I'll

leave this jeep with you. Use it as you will.'

The open-handed concession put an unexpected dampener on Bernadette's steam. She glared at him suspiciously.

The black eyes danced back at her. 'Two?' he prompted, and his mouth pursed in that deliberately sensual way he had.

'Two!' Bernadette grated, determined not to let him get under her skin. 'I didn't come here to . . . to become your personal possession. So if you think I'll allow you to make love to me, you'd better think again, Danton, because whatever else happens . . . that won't!'

The twinkle was swallowed up by a dark mockery. '"To thine own self be true," Bernadette,' he recited in his soft, taunting voice.

Her chin lifted scornfully. 'That's one thing I am! And you'd better believe it!'

One black eyebrow arched in challenge. 'Then don't deny the inevitable truth that we will be lovers.'

'It's not inevitable!'

'You know it,' he mocked. 'You've always known it. Just as I have. From the first time we met.'

The outrageous statement stunned Bernadette for a moment. 'How ridiculous!' she managed weakly, as her mind spiralled into confusion.

She had certainly recognised her vulnerability to Danton's sexual magnetism, acknowledged the danger of being seduced by him, but had she ever consciously accepted that they would be lovers? Did she actually want that? The idea certainly had its appeal, but . . .

'That is utterly ridiculous!' she repeated more firmly.

Danton sliced her a look that suggested she was only fooling herself, but he made no further comment. The boys arrived with her luggage and he directed that the suitcases be placed in the back of the jeep. As soon as they were in, he started the engine and took off along a dirt road that was little more than a track.

Bernadette shelved her soul-searching for the time being. One thing was certain. She was not about to jump into bed with Danton Fayette just because he desired her! If she made such a choice . . . it would be because she wanted to. In the meantime, there were more immediate problems facing her . . . like the hut she had to live in!

They travelled a few hundred metres before coming to a row of thatched-roof bungalows that bordered the beach. They were shaded by trees and palms, and hibiscus hedges ran between them, affording them privacy from each other. Bernadette felt mightily relieved when Danton turned off the track and parked the jeep beside one of them.

The 'hut' was obviously of native construction: piers and posts from coconut trees; walls of bamboo; and the thatch was thick layers of pandanus leaves; but she could see that the floor was of tongued and grooved hardwood, so it looked like a fairly decent habitation. More than decent, Bernadette had to admit, when Danton led her inside.

The pitched roof was very high, and open to the air at both the gabled ends, allowing a breeze to flow through and cool the place. The front room was very large, perhaps seven metres wide and four metres deep. It was furnished as a sitting-room with cane armchairs and sofas that featured brightly patterned cushions. Colourful scatter-rugs softened the floor. A huge basket of tropical fruit sat on a large coffee-table. A short hallway ran from the centre of the back wall and to the right of this was a sink and refrigerator and a row of cupboards.

Danton walked down the hallway, opening the doors to either side of it. One led to a well-appointed bathroom with completely modern plumbing, the other to a spacious bedroom that contained a wall of built-in cupboards, a dressing-table, a well-stocked bookcase, and a king-size bed.

'Satisfied with your accommodation?' Danton asked, his eyes teasing merrily.

'It's very comfortable, thank you,' Bernadette said, leading straight back to the living-room, away from the bed. 'But where do I cook?'

'I won't have you doing any menial tasks. You'll find snack-foods in the cupboards and fridge if you get hungry. Tanoa and her mother, Rosina, will bring you your meals. I'll introduce them to you when you join me for lunch.'

'How do I go about finding you? I don't know where you live,' Bernadette reminded him.

'Easy. You simply walk next door. The hut to your left.' He grinned and strolled out to the deep porch that ran across the front of the bungalow. 'I'll get your luggage and bring it in.'

'But . . .' He had already stepped off the porch and she hurriedly followed him. 'Why don't you live in your house?'

He turned a laughing face to her. 'It would interfere with our privacy, because the plantation manager lives there. I'm sure you'll like this arrangement much better.' He cocked his head to one side in musing speculation. 'One day—if you decide that I retain the island—I may build something more to your fancy. But for the present, this suits me fine.'

Bernadette's heart sank as the full ramifications of the situation hit her. Danton was going to do everything in his power to seduce her, and he underlined the proximity angle with flagrant disregard for her feelings on the matter.

'I think it would only be forty paces from your porch to mine,' he continued, his eyes deliberately measuring the distance before dancing back to hers. 'Or vice versa. We are what you might call close neighbours. Such a small distance to cross . . . it shouldn't waste much of your time . . . or mine.'

Bernadette held her tongue, but she seethed over

the amusement he had had at her expense. She wondered how many women he had done this to . . . calling this charming bungalow a hut so they would expect the worst; providing them with a separate residence that was right within pouncing distance. And there was no doubt that at present she was the next one on his list.

She watched him go to the jeep for her luggage, and felt even hotter with the thought that she would always be conscious of his presence so close to her. He started lifting out her suitcases, the muscles of his back rippling as he took their weight. Bernadette wrenched her gaze away and returned to the sitting-room.

Whether it was Danton who was sending up her temperature, or the tropical heat of the day, she didn't know, but even her head felt damp with perspiration. She took off her hat and flung it on to the nearest armchair, then slid her arms out of the long-sleeved coat. It was about to join the hat, but on second thoughts Bernadette carried it to the bedroom to hang it in the cupboard.

The hanging-space was not completely empty. A colourful range of pareu cloths had been placed there, apparently for her use. On the floor below them were several pairs of pretty thongs, their straps decorated by shells.

'In this climate pareus are far more suitable than fashion clothes, Bernadette. You won't find the heat so uncomfortable in them.'

Danton's voice startled her. She had meant to be out of the bedroom before he brought her luggage in. He set down her bags, effectively blocking the doorway, and suddenly there was an infinitely dangerous gleam in his teasing black eyes.

'So . . . alone at last,' he drawled.

'No!' she said sharply, trying to quell her inner panic as he stepped towards her.

'I've waited a long time for this.'

She glared defiance at him as he closed the short distance between them. 'You wouldn't use force, Danton.'

He shook his head. 'I won't have to. I'm sure you're not an innocent virgin any longer, Bernadette.'

Hot colour whipped into her cheeks at the reference to their first meeting so long ago. 'So what if I'm not?' she admitted. 'I don't . . .'

'Then stop fighting with me.'

'Sex is not the answer to everything!' she snapped fiercely. 'It's not the answer to anything!'

'Are you sure?' he mocked.

'Yes, I'm sure! I've experienced it before. All in the name of love,' she cried bitterly, remembering the man who had deceived her into believing him . . . for a short while.

Danton's languid mask slipped. His face tightened and his eyes glittered with a deep, savage anger. 'Damn the fool! But don't make the mistake of living on with what's happened in the past, Bernadette. At best, that is remaining stagnant . . . standing still . . . and life is about moving forward, not looking back as you have done.'

He lifted his hand and lightly squeezed her

shoulder as his eyes bored into hers with purposeful intensity. 'This is no mistake. You want me as I want you. As I said, "To thine own self be true," Bernadette. Live up to your principles. Don't live a life of self-deceit. Tell me what you really feel . . . the desire curling through you right now . . . the need to know and feel all there can be between us.'

His arm hooked around her waist. Undisguised and undiluted hunger blazed from his eyes, and before Bernadette could recover from the shock of such raw passion he had swept her body hard against his.

She slapped her hands up against his chest in a frantic effort to push away, but he kept her relentlessly pinned to him. 'I don't need you!' she cried in desperate protest. 'I don't need anyone!'

'Is that so, Bernadette?' he asked softly, dangerously.

'Please . . .' She was shaking inside, quivering with a devastating awareness of the powerful thighs pressed against hers, the hard masculinity that was stirring a terrifying weakness. Even her voice sounded furred with uncertainty as she fought to resist what he was doing to her. 'Please go away . . . leave me alone!'

His grip on her slackened fractionally and, sensing a crack in his arrogant confidence, Bernadette wildly snatched at the chance to break it. 'I don't want you, Danton!'

It was a mistake! His eyes hardened into firm

resolve and his face tightened into rigid lines of purpose. 'The problem with your mouth, Bernadette, is that it keeps uttering meaningless words when it should be doing much more marvellous things.'

She tried to jerk her head away, but his hand closed around it, denying her escape. She dug her nails into his shoulders, but he took no notice. His mouth closed over hers with a hard, plundering pressure that would not acknowledge any resistance. She was forced into submitting to the throbbing need of his lips and a mad, wilful excitement began coursing through her veins, undermining what little control she had left.

He kissed her until she forgot she was supposed to keep struggling against him. Her mouth opened to the hard, driving passion of his and welcomed the intimate invasion, responded with wild abandonment to every attack it made on her swimming senses. Her hands slithered wantonly over his shoulders, around his neck, into the thick, riotous curls that wound through her fingers. She pressed her breasts into the exciting warmth of his naked chest. And, just as her body exulted in surrendering to the sensations that Danton had generated, he pulled away from her.

Bernadette opened her eyes in bewilderment at the abrupt withdrawal. His head was thrown back, his breathing harsh. Then he looked down at her with hard, glittering eyes.

'Now tell me you don't want me! Deny the evidence of your senses . . . and know that you lie,

Bernadette!'

She stared back at him, too shaken to speak, and hating him for arousing her to the point where he could so coldly and deliberately use her mindless response to him as a weapon against her.

His mouth curled mockingly at her continued silence. 'It's not going to stop here, Bernadette. Make your mind up to what's going to happen in the next thirty days. I'll not take no for an answer. I'll keep kissing you until you surrender, so sooner or later you'll have to face up to the truth.'

He released her, and at the abrupt loss of his support Bernadette rocked on her feet.

'I'll leave you now . . . to savour the same frustration I feel,' Danton said on his way to the door. He paused to cast a searing look back at her. 'When you're ready for lunch, you know where to come.'

'I'm staying here!' she flung at him, furious with his cat-and-mouse tactics.

'Fine,' he said carelessly. 'I'll send it over to you. But don't think you can hide all month, Bernadette. Either from me . . . or yourself.'

And with that parting shot he left her alone to review the situation again, having ripped away any delusions Bernadette had about controlling anything.

'The most dangerous man I know,' her father had said, and Bernadette wished she had taken more heed of those words. She sank down on the bed, feeling hopelessly defeated. There was no point in lying to herself. However hateful he was, however bitterly she resented his power over her, Danton Fayette was a force to be reckoned with.

The question was, how best to cope with it, because on one point he was absolutely right. There was no escape from facing him sooner or later.

CHAPTER NINE

NEEDING some soothing from her anger and frustration, Bernadette stripped off her hot clothes and stepped across the hallway into the bathroom. The shower stall was luxurious enough to hold two people in comfort. Very convenient, she thought sourly, and wondered if she should simply give in to Danton and save herself the strain of trying to repress her own treacherous impulses.

The temptation was strong—on a purely physical level no one had ever excited her as much—but her mind fiercely rebelled against filling the position of current lover in Danton Fayette's life. And she didn't want to give him the satisfaction of adding her to his list.

That same sense of pride burned through Bernadette an hour later, when a young Polynesian girl arrived on the front porch with a tray of food. She introduced herself as Tanoa and explained that she and her mother looked after Danton and his guests. Bernadette cynically wondered what the 'looking after' entailed.

Tanoa's pareu was knotted at the hip, leaving an expanse of lissom leg on view, not to mention a naked torso that any woman would envy. She looked about seventeen and was as lovely as any young girl could be: huge, dark velvet eyes, a nose that was only slightly broad, full, sensual lips, a glorious mane of black hair which fell to her waist, and smooth honey-brown skin that gleamed like silk. She wore a crown of red hibiscus blooms that matched the print in her pareu, and a many-stranded necklace of tiny white shells that almost—but not quite—hid her beautiful bare breasts.

Bernadette couldn't imagine any man not feeling some spark of desire for the girl. Had Tanoa shared Danton's bed? Probably, she thought. Perhaps every woman he asked did, she added, feeling slightly hysterical with the knowledge that she herself was hopelessly susceptible to the same desire. And, even worse, what she was feeling towards Tanoa was rank jealousy.

Bernadette tried to clamp down on her disturbing feelings and make conversation with the girl as she set the lunch dishes on the table—a chicken salad, sliced pineapple and melon, a jug of iced fruit juice. Tanoa seemed extremely shy. Bernadette could hardly draw a word out of her, but the girl kept throwing her covert little glances that made Bernadette feel more and more self-conscious.

She had put on a peasant skirt and a loose off-the-shoulder blouse after her shower, and coiled her hair on top of her head for coolness. A lot of the clothes she had brought were completely unsuitable for the situation she now found herself in, and she had left them in her suitcases, but surely the skirt and blouse were not particularly remarkable?

'Why are you looking at me like that?' she finally demanded in exasperation. 'Is there something odd about me, Tanoa?'

'You are so beautiful, I cannot help it,' the girl replied artlessly.

'You think *I'm* beautiful?' Bernadette squeaked incredulously.

The girl nodded with vigorous conviction. 'Your eyes are as blue as the sky. And your hair is like sunrays in the morning. I know I am lucky that my skin is not so dark as others', but to have pale skin like you . . .' She sighed in envy. 'Our people prize that very much. Even those that bleach their skin cannot get it as pale as yours.'

Bernadette shook her head, absolutely dumbfounded. Then, as the irony of the situation hit her, she began to laugh.

'Most women I know would give their eye-teeth to look like you, Tanoa,' she said, then couldn't resist asking, 'Doesn't Danton tell you how lovely you are?'

The girl looked puzzled. 'Mr Fayette doesn't talk of such things to me.'

Bernadette's mouth curled. 'How remiss of him!'

'He is very busy with his writing,' Tanoa said placatingly.

He surely didn't have that much correspondence to do here? Bernadette thought sourly. 'Even at night?' she said, her voice laced with scepticism.

'I do not know. Mama and I go home after we serve the evening meal,' came the innocent reply.

Bernadette was shamed by it. Apparently Danton was not as profligate as she had imagined, at least not on Te Enata, or Tanoa would surely have remarked on any liaison she knew about. 'Is there some special man you like?' she asked, prompting for more information.

The girl's face lit up. 'Oh, yes! I've got Momo. He is very handsome, and the best dancer on the island. You will see him tonight at the *Tamaaraa*.'

'*Tamaaraa?*' Bernadette questioned. 'Is that a place on the island?'

'Oh, no! It is a great feast with singing and dancing. We are having it in your honour to welcome you to our island. And I am going to dance with Momo. He is very exciting. I am the envy of all the girls to have him as my lover.'

'Your lover,' Bernadette repeated, somewhat dazed by the girl's openness. 'Do you intend to marry him?'

Tanoa shrugged. 'I have not thought about it. I am only sixteen.'

'What if you have a baby?'

Tanoa smiled. 'I would like that. My friend Marita is having a baby soon.'

'Is she married?'

'Oh, no! She is young like me. We will choose husbands later,' she said complacently.

Bernadette decided to leave probing this subject to some other time. She was aware that the Polynesian society made no attempt to repress sexuality in the younger generation; that the youth were actively encouraged to acquire as much sexual knowledge and skill as possible before marriage. She wondered what it would be like to feel so easy about it, to enjoy uninhibited sexual pleasure without any moral or emotional questions involved.

Impossible for someone like herself, she thought ruefully, but how much time had Danton spent on this island with his grandfather in the growing-up years? If his attitude towards sex and sensuality had been moulded here, was she right to judge it as bad?

She shook her head, irritated that she should be so preoccupied with him, and needing some respite from the questions that kept circling her mind. She asked Tanoa if she would accompany her around the island in the jeep after lunch and the girl happily agreed.

They set off an hour later and Bernadette was relieved to get away from the hut and put more distance between herself and the man she found so disturbing.

Tanoa suggested they stop at the large huts near the end of the pier. 'The general store, and the markets and the clinic,' she said proudly.

'Tell me about the clinic,' Bernadette prompted, recalling that Danton had said there was no doctor on the island.

'It is where special medicines are kept,' Tanoa explained. 'Mama Cantineaux, the old one who lived here on the plantation, used to give out the medicines and fix things. She showed Ariitea how to do it, so if anyone is sick or hurt, they can come to the clinic.'

Danton's grandmother, Bernadette surmised, and wondered how the Frenchwoman had liked living here.

The general store was precisely that: everything from basic foodstuffs to frying pans and hardware tools and dress-cloths. The array of goods was amazingly old-fashioned and fascinating, and Bernadette shook her head at the contrast to a supermarket at home.

Next door to it was a huge barn-like hall, completely open on the side, looking out over the lagoon. This was filled with local market goods: trestle tables loaded with fresh fruit and vegetables; hats and baskets; necklaces and bracelets made of shells; wooden carvings.

'The fish catch will be brought in later,' Tanoa said, obviously glorying in her role as Bernadette's escort and interpreter. All the native women were intensely curious about their visitor and wanted to know everything about her.

While they were clustered around Bernadette asking questions, a group of young boys came running up from the lagoon to report that one of them had cut his foot on a sharp piece of coral. Ariitea ordered the bleeding boy to the clinic, and Bernadette asked if she might look at the wound, explaining that she was a doctor and might be able to help.

'*Taote!*'

The cry was echoed around the group and everyone wanted to watch Bernadette doing a doctor's job. As it turned out, the boy's foot was cut badly enough to require stitching, and Bernadette sent Tanoa off to get the medical bag from the hut.

She washed the wound clean of all sand and grit. Ariitea produced a bottle of disinfectant and bandages, ready for application. By then Tanoa had returned, and Bernadette's audience 'oohed' and 'aahed' as several stitches pulled the gashed edges of skin neatly together.

Ariitea did her job with a bandage and everyone clapped the boy as he hobbled off, swaggering with importance at having suffered through such an extraordinary thing. Ariitea enthusiastically invited Bernadette to check over everything in the clinic, and proudly showed off the contents of a well-stocked first aid cupboard. She happily invited the *taote* to help any time Bernadette liked.

Finally Tanoa drew Bernadette away, suggesting that she might like to see the *Ahimaa* being prepared for the evening's feast. Bernadette had suddenly turned from a curiosity to a celebrity, and she and Tanoa were trailed down the beach by a growing number of women and children who wanted to meet or simply to look closely at the *taote* who had come among them.

The men who were preparing the *Ahimaa* were delighted to find themselves the centre of attention, and they showed off like children as Tanoa explained how the earth-oven worked.

At the bottom of the hole was a layer of volcanic rocks, already preheated. The men lay fresh banana leaves over these to form a lining for the oven. Then came carefully wrapped bundles of food: chicken, pork, fish, taro, breadfruit, sweet potatoes and numerous other vegetables. These were covered by more banana leaves. Then the men shovelled hot lava rocks on to the top and covered them with burlap bags and earth.

'Three . . . four hours,' one of them informed Bernadette with a triumphant grin.

'How do you say thank you in your language?' Bernadette asked Tanoa.

'Mauruuuru roa.'

Bernadette did her best to repeat it. Everyone laughed delightedly and clapped her attempt. Bernadette laughed too. 'I'll have to practise it,' she said, and received happy cries of encouragement.

As they passed the markets on their way back to the jeep, a group of women confronted Bernadette with gifts; a blue and pink pareu in a soft fine cotton, a fresh lei of gardenias and a matching lei *upo'o* to crown her hair.

'Tamaaraa,' they all chorused.

'For you to wear tonight,' Tanoa explained.

'But . . .' Bernadette bit down on her tongue. The older women had their pareus knotted over their shoulders, and it wouldn't hurt her to go modestly 'native' for one night. She didn't want to offend them. *'Mauruuuru roa,'* she tried again, and the women beamed with pleasure.

All in all it had been an extremely pleasant and relaxing afternoon, Bernadette thought as she drove back to her bungalow. The islanders were open and friendly, just as Danton had said. Bernadette looked forward to learning more about them. And at least that was one safe topic of conversation she could use with Danton this evening.

If anything could be said to be safe with him!

And nothing was!

Tanoa spent some considerable time tutoring Bernadette in the ways of the pareu. The Polynesian girl couldn't understand why Bernadette insisted that her breasts be covered, but she was persuaded that it had to be so. Bernadette was not about to go to the *Tamaaraa* dressed as an open invitation for Danton to pursue his objective.

Eventually she was satisfied with one of the styles Tanoa showed her. The cloth was centred at her back, its ends brought under her arms and tied at the front; then the material hanging from the knot was swathed across her breasts and tied again at her back. The end result was a cool strapless shift that was very feminine and flattering.

Nevertheless, however much Bernadette argued to herself that the pareu was as modest as a sundress, she felt uncomfortably aware of how fragile a covering it was when Danton called at her hut to take her to the *Tamaaraa*. She had brushed her long hair out of its thick coil in order to wear the head lei properly, and as Danton's dark gaze roved over her Bernadette's satisfaction in her appearance instantly churned into something far more electric.

He had changed his red pareu for a royal blue one, and he wore a lei of gardenias. Somehow the floral garland seemed to emphasise his powerful masculinity, and Bernadette could not forget how his body had felt against hers, nor the mindless desire he could stir whether she wanted it or not.

She stood at the entrance to the hallway, he stood poised at her front door, his hand clutching its frame tightly as if to stop himself from advancing further. His eyes seemed to burn up the distance between them, devouring every detail of her with an intensity that sent a flush of heat through Bernadette's entire body.

He spoke in a husky murmur. 'You look even more lovely now than you did at eighteen.'

The black eyes weren't teasing or mocking, and Bernadette felt even more defenceless against the unexpected change in his manner. She tried to shield herself with anger, remembering his outrageous presumption that she had always wanted them to be lovers.

'That night at the Mandarin Hotel . . . how can you believe I wanted you? I told you very plainly what I thought of you, Danton,' she burst out in agitated protest.

'You might have spoken the conviction of your

soul, Bernadette, but your eyes wanted to reach me, and when we danced . . .'

And the knowledge was there, gleaming in his eyes, a memory that Bernadette wished he had forgotten.

'A man always knows when a woman cannot help reacting to him. On that night, it was so with you. Your cheeks were flushed with excitement, your breathing so fast and shallow that you became light-headed. Your pulse beat like a drum. But in the ways of love you were young and innocent and artless.'

She hated to think she had been so obvious. Although she had felt strongly drawn to him, it had certainly been against her will, and the need to defy his judgement sprang to her tongue.

'How you change the facts, Danton!' she scoffed. 'If that is the truth . . . if I was so innocent . . . why didn't you take advantage of me? How can you explain that away?'

His mouth curled with soft irony. 'Because afterwards you would have hated me for it. You needed the time . . . to do what you had to do. There was no other alternative. I had to give you that time.'

Bernadette stared at him, torn between belief and disbelief. 'Why? Why should you do that?' she demanded, needing to understand why he was doing this to her now if he had denied his desire for her then.

The languid mask of mockery slid back into place. 'You can make love to a young girl. You can only have a woman as a lover,' he drawled, his eyes filcking their sharp taunt at her. 'You are now a woman . . .'

'What you're insinuating is crazy!' she insisted.

He shrugged. 'Six years ago you told me what you wanted to achieve with your life. You wanted to be a doctor and help those in need. I know you do voluntary work for a women's shelter, and for the Autistic Children's Association as well. You sell the cars your father presents to you . . . give the proceeds over to your favourite charities. You offer your services to unfortunates who cannot pay. You have achieved most of the things you told me . . .'

He paused. Bernadette was deeply disturbed by the amount of detail he knew about her, but she held her tongue, waiting for the punchline she sensed was coming.

'Now you're ready for love,' he stated with arrogant confidence.

'That's all you can think about, isn't it?' Bernadette lashed out at him with scornful fury. 'It was the same when we first met in Hong Kong. All you could think about was love, love, love! As if there was nothing else worth doing or having or caring about. You haven't changed one bit, Danton.'

'In that respect . . . no,' he said. 'I haven't changed.'

'You say you wanted me then, but your desire was so transient, Danton, that you were with another woman the very next morning. And don't deny it, because you know I saw you with her in the hotel lobby!' she accused in bitter challenge. 'I'll never be ready for your on-one-moment-and-off-the-next kind of love!'

'So you were jealous,' he said with an infuriating ring of satisfaction. 'I was in Hong Kong on business, Bernadette, and that woman was purely a business connection. Nothing to do with sex at all. You simply preferred to believe the worst of me, so you did. It was easier than admitting what you really wanted.'

'Can't you see we're opposites?' she cried desperately, struggling to stave off the calm relentlessness that flowed from him. 'We could never share anything, Danton!'

'Perhaps . . .' he said slowly. 'I hear you've already started your good works here. So I wonder what will happen when the big test comes. When you have to make the decision about the island.' His lips moved provocatively. 'Will you be true to your principles then, Bernadette? Deciding for the good of the islanders? Or will you decide . . . against the person you think I am . . . and for the father you want to have?'

Bernadette shook her head in a bewildered daze. 'You constructed this . . . this test—is that what it is?—because I hurt your ego six years ago?'

He gave a soft laugh that prickled her skin, and slowly strolled across the room towards her. But his eyes belied the laugh and the casual manner. They burnt with the fire of intense and totally committed purpose.

'Not because you hurt my ego, Bernadette. You didn't even bruise my ego. But you fascinated me. You enticed me. You drew me to you like a magnet. You still do. And I want to know . . . of what steel you are made!'

Bernadette swallowed hard, desperate not to show the effect he had on her. It was worse than being a mesmerised rabbit. Every nerve in her body was tingling in anticipation, urging her to move forward, meet him half-way. The power of his attraction was frightening. She had to keep him away from her.

'And what are you, Danton?' she sliced back at him. 'What are you made of? Tell me that!'

He smiled. 'That's your voyage of discovery, Bernadette. I hope this time around you may not find me the purveyor of evil you once did.'

She stared at the man who had fascinated her, enticed her, drawn her like a magnet—and still did! He was lazily self-assured, infernally clever, damnably attractive, and quite possibly completely mad!

And she could feel the trap closing in on her . . . tighter and tighter. He was pulling her into an intense little world where only she and he existed, locked in combat.

He reached across the brief space between them and took her hand in his, the strong brown fingers pressing relentless possession. But he did not try to draw her into an embrace . . . or kiss her.

'Come. Let us go to the feast. We'll walk along

the beach.'

The relief of not being kissed was instantly followed by a pang of . . . regret? Bernadette tried to crush the feeling, deny it, but in all honesty, although it was frightening to be unable to control what he did to her body, there was a dreadful fascination in the way it responded to him.

Feeling more confused than ever, Bernadette accompanied him without resistance. Which was undoubtedly what he intended, she thought. Confuse and conquer!

They walked up the beach in silence, both immersed in their own thoughts. Bernadette was annoyed with herself for having fallen into step beside him. She should have driven the jeep . . . let him walk by himself! But here she was . . . being dragged along by a force she had a great deal of trouble resisting.

Of course she could always pull her hand out of his, but she was not sure she wanted to. And yet, she didn't want Danton to think she was acquiescing in his intentions concerning her. On the other hand, she would be safe for the next hour or two while they were at the *Tamaaraa*, surrounded by the island people. What he intended afterwards . . .

The thought conjured up a range of possibilities that didn't bear dwelling on. Bernadette needed more information and, since Danton wasn't volunteering any, she had to ask.

'Tanoa said there will be singing and dancing after the feast tonight,' she remarked. 'Is there anything else on the programme after that?'

'Yes.' Danton sliced her a glittering look. 'You will see the *tamure* . . . which is the most erotic dance in the world.'

'I'm sure you're the expert on such things,' she retorted acidly.

His eyes mocked her sarcasm. 'You may judge for yourself.'

A little shiver ran down Bernadette's spine. Was it fear or excitement? How could she hate a man and want him at the same time? And what was she going to do about it? She couldn't keep shelving the question. She needed an answer before they walked back down this beach tonight. Because there was no doubt that Danton was going to demand one!

CHAPTER TEN

No SOONER had they passed the pier than a happy party of Polynesians swarmed around them. They were led up to what was obviously a place of honour: a large mat woven from pandanus leaves and set under a tree at the back of a grassy clearing just above the beach. Bernadette noticed that everyone, including the men, wore leis.

The food from the *Ahimaa* was served with great ceremony. Delicious odours filled the air. The feast was an unforgettable experience for Bernadette: the pork was succulent; the marinated fish melted in her mouth; the different tastes of smoke-flavoured breadfruit, *Fafa*, the Tahitian spinach, *Fe'i*, a red banana, and other vegetables that Danton explained were staple foods of the Polynesians. Finally they were served with a virtual rainbow of tropical fruit, and Bernadette sighed her satisfaction.

Danton smiled that slow, lazy smile that seemed to curl around her heart. 'The best is yet to come.'

Bernadette wrenched her eyes away from him and fastened them on the natives who were lighting torches around the clearing. The sun had set and the twilight was going fast. And Bernadette still hadn't come to any decision about Danton.

A loud cheer went up from the crowd of spectators as a group of men appeared with an assortment of musical instruments: skin and wooden drums and a couple of ukeleles. They set themselves up to one side and began playing short little solos, as if to introduce themselves.

A flock of women streamed into the clearing. They sat down, equally spaced apart in rows.

'This is an *apirima*, a dance with the hands,' Danton remarked.

The ukelele gave the main accompaniment. The graceful gestures and the way the women swayed their bodies to the music enchanted Bernadette. Everyone sang, and their voices were delicately sweet and musical. The song ended and the drums started a frenetic beat. The women fled from the clearing as a group of men leapt into it.

Gone were their pareus! They wore brief white lap-cloths. Long shredded leaves hung from reed circlets around their necks, and arms, and just below their knees.

They began an incredibly skilful dance where they balanced on the balls of their feet in a semi-crouched position and moved their legs apart and back together with amazing rapidity; the strong muscles of their thighs rippling with the movement which grew more and more mesmerising as Bernadette watched.

The drums beat faster and faster, then suddenly broke off. The men leapt high in the air with a loud cry and pulled back to form a circle. All except one, who remained in the centre.

The men slapped their thighs in a slowly accelerating rhythm. The wooden drums started clacking and a young woman—Tanoa!—moved slowly into the clearing, her arms gracefully extended, her hips rotating provocatively. A garland of flowers fixed to the edge of her low-slung pareu accentuated the vibrant sensuality of her body. The man had to be Momo, Tanoa's lover, but as she danced around him he pretended to ignore her, despite her most tantalising efforts to draw his attention.

Bernadette glanced sharply at Danton to see what effect Tanoa's dance was having on him, but she found him watching her, not the dancer.

'She's . . . very skilful,' Bernadette observed, feeling constrained to make some comment.

'Trained from birth . . . to know and enjoy being a woman,' Danton answered.

While she had trained to be a doctor and was less of a woman for it? Bernadette turned away from the taunt in his eyes, disdaining a reply, not wanting to acknowledge . . . anything!

Momo snapped out of his pose of indifference and responded to Tanoa's provocative invitation. He broke into the rapid thigh movement that was suddenly made explosively erotic with the rhythmic thrust of his loins.

Bernadette sucked in her breath at the blatantly sexual connotations. Tanoa replied to him with a frenzied hip-movement that was equally explicit. They danced together, face to face but not touching, goading each other into a faster, faster rhythm—all the drums driving into a wild, intoxicating beat. Other girls swept into the circle enticing the men to leap up and join them. Their bodies gleamed in the torchlight as they moved with a frenzied, primitive passion.

Bernadette could not tear her eyes away. She could feel her heart pounding faster with the drums, knew that the sheer eroticism of the dance was stirring an answering fever in her own blood . . . a sheer, wanton desire to be part of it, to throw off the shackles of civilisation and be consumed with the wildness of the moment.

The drums rose to a shattering crescendo and then stopped. The dancers gave an exultant shout and ran off into the darkness of the trees beyond the clearing, the girls leading, the men chasing.

Every nerve-end in Bernadette's body quivered as Danton brushed his lips over her bare shoulder. She jerked around to face him and the black eyes bored into hers.

'The show is over,' he murmured. 'It's time for us to leave.'

He knew, of course. He knew exactly what she felt. It was why he had brought her here . . . to stamp such basic instincts into her consciousness.

Bernadette stumbled to her feet and forced her shaky legs to walk down the beach, not once looking at Danton until they were well past the pier. She was all too aware of the man accompanying her, matching his step to hers, haunting her with thoughts and feelings she could not repress however hard she tried.

And why deny herself the experience of making love with him? Maybe it would be memorable. At least she would have the satisfaction of knowing how good or bad it was. To thine own self be true, she thought wildly, wanting him more than she had ever wanted any man in her life.

She stopped walking, resenting the power of his strong sexuality even as it drew a decision from her. She couldn't fight him off. Not for another month. And she wanted him. The desire he evoked in her—and had done so six long years ago—was more than the rest of all mankind had ever done. She had fought against him and lost. Was bound to lose. But that was no reason why he should get any pleasure from her submission. And he would not!

He had halted beside her, and she swung on him like a caged lioness defending its cubs. 'All right! If this is what you've schemed for . . . if this is what you want . . . then you can have your just deserts, Danton! Go ahead! Do it to me. Get it over and done with and out of the way! And I promise you I'll hate you for it!' she said fiercely, her hands already working at the knot behind her back.

Danton said nothing. She saw him tense as she pulled the end of the pareu free and unwound it from her body. She tossed it on the sand and stepped out of the remaining scrap of cloth, tossing it away with equal contempt. The leis she hurled into the water to float away. Then she stood proudly before him, her stance one of taunting challenge as the soft breeze caressed her nakedness.

'What's the matter, Danton? Isn't this going to plan? Or do you think I'm no good at it?' She didn't know what possessed her to say such things, but they ripped off her tongue and something inside her exulted in goading him.

'Are you?'

The words gravelled out of his throat and she knew he was not unaffected by her actions, that he was strained to the limits of his control.

She laughed out of sheer heady excitement, intoxicated with the power she could wield over him. 'That's the risk you take, isn't it, Danton? Is it worth it . . . to gamble all this for the sake of sexual passion?'

He didn't reply. He lifted off his lei and tossed it after hers; untied his pareu and let it drop to the sand at his feet.

He wore nothing else, and Bernadette's stomach clenched at the sight of his flagrant manhood, as carelessly exposed as she had exposed herself, and he stood in front of her with the same proud challenge she had thrown him.

'I will not be dismissed as easily as that, Bernadette,' he said, his voice low and vibrant with feeling. 'The desire we have for each other runs too deep to be sated in one night.'

His arm lifted. A nerve-rending wave of trepidation hit Bernadette, but she stood her ground. His hand curled softly around her shoulder. Her pulse leapt at his touch. He moved closer to her, leaving only a bare breathing space between them. His eyes burned into hers with probing intensity and Bernadette felt she was drowning in their black depths, but she held her own gaze steady, defiant to the last second of submitting any part of her independence.

'I'm not surrendering to you, Danton. I'll never do that. I'm simply taking what I want tonight. Because I want you,' she insisted wildly.

His hand slid down her arm, curled around her hand and slowly lifted it to his shoulder. The warmth of his naked flesh seemed to burn through her palm, and she would have recoiled from the contact but for his hand covering hers, keeping it still. He spoke in a low, husky murmur.

'This must last, Bernadette. I have waited too long.'

His other hand gently touched her waist. Her skin quivered.

'What are you after?' she asked, bewildered by his restraint.

'To hold you,' he answered. 'To make you love me.'

He released his grasp on her hand and very gently drew her body against his. The slow, gradual pressure of her soft breasts against the firm wall of his chest brought a flood of sensitivity; the meeting of their lower bodies was explosive. It drove the breath from Bernadette's lungs. Need cried through every nerve-ending in her body. In sheer reflex action to the erotic excitement, she tried to jerk away.

Danton's hand was unrelenting, keeping her pinned to every powerful muscle of his body. He moved against her slowly, until he felt her accept the contact and the strangeness of it melted into familiarity. He began to stroke her back: long, slow caresses that made her shiver with pleasure.

'Let this last for eternity, Bernadette,' he whispered. 'Let it be the most magical moment of our lives. Listen to the water lapping the sand . . . enjoy the softness of the breeze . . . look at the stars . . . feel the feeling of my body . . . every yearning pulse of my desire for you . . . yours for me . . . and know it is part of nature for all of time.'

She didn't understand him, nor what he was doing to her. But for once she didn't care. She was tired of the fighting, the need to be alert every minute, to guard and fend away. And what he did . . . and said . . . felt right.

It was strange . . . simply to be held like this. No one had ever done it before, never in her entire life, not even in caring or comfort when she was a child. And the men who had held her in other embraces had always wanted something from her.

Danton did, too. There was no disguising his excitement. But he was in no hurry to satisfy his desire. He stroked her hair with a soft tenderness that was soothing and infinitely pleasant. She sighed and rested her head on his shoulder. She liked the feel of his body. It was strong, supportive, secure and warm.

She ran her fingers tentatively, experimentally, over his back. Muscles contracted rigidly under her touch. Otherwise he didn't move, and Bernadette was emboldened enough to hug him as he hugged her. His body shuddered, and he held her more tightly.

They stood there, entwined in a togetherness that could not be more intimate. She was aware of every part of her body, and his, sensitive to even the most minute shift in contact and intensely excited by it. Her skin felt alive. The more Danton stroked her back with his featherlight fingertips, the more exquisitely sensitive it became. The pleasure of it was greater than anything she had previously known. She wanted it to go on forever.

She hadn't realised what she was doing until she had done it . . . moving her mouth across his broad shoulder, kissing the curve under his ear. She felt his chest expand with a quick intake of breath and a delicious tingle spread through her breasts.

His fingers wound through her hair and gently pulled her head back. His face was sharply etched in savage lines of restraint, but his lips were gentle as he bent to kiss her temples, her eyelids, her nose, her cheeks—soft, sensual kisses, unhurried, undemanding.

'Kiss me properly,' she pleaded huskily, her voice seeming to struggle from a great distance, her mind disorientated, hazy.

His mouth searched hers with slow, controlled sensuality that stopped short of passion, until she responded uninhibitedly, seeking to know him as he was knowing her. A hoarse cry was stifled in his throat, but she felt the explosive thrust of his body. Her head was thrown back as he broke the violent passion of their kiss to plunder her face and throat with his lips in a yearning need for her that stirred a wild flood of response.

He swept her up in his arms, carried her a few driven steps, then lowered her on to the soft cotton of the pareu she had discarded. She didn't understand herself, why she could feel like this, but she wasn't afraid of Danton any more. There was no intention to hurt. She was sure of that.

He bent to kiss her breasts and she arched in sheer wanton pleasure. Her hands raked through his hair and stroked over his shoulders, and, when his head moved lower to run soft little kisses over the inner sides of her thighs, her whole body quivered with delight. He caressed her legs, rubbed his cheek across her stomach, kissed her with a sensuality that Bernadette had never even thought to experience, and it excited her into touching him, wanting to know, to taste, to give him the same wonderful sensations.

She felt the tremors that ran through him and exulted in them, heard his breathing quicken and knew the heady power of exciting him, drew his mouth to hers . . . and there was no more control. They kissed with devouring need, their bodies sliding together, intuitively seeking a deeper, more intense possession of each other.

Every nerve-ending in Bernadette's body seemed to be reaching out to be touched, and as Danton entered her a pulsating wave of sensation swept right through her in a swelling roll. She clung to him in mindless wonder, and with every movement inside her came another wave of ecstatic feeling, swaying, crashing, tumbling, bathing her in swirls of melting sweetness. It was like an exquisite dance with a wild, erotic rhythm . . . slow . . . fast . . . explosive . . . there was no movement—no refinement or nuance of movement—that Danton did not know . . . and then finally a euphoric floating, while warm arms cradled her and soothed the exquisite aftermath of delicious sensitivity.

Gradually she became aware of the soft breeze caressing her skin . . . the lapping of water on the sand . . . the stars in the sky . . . the feel of his body under hers . . . the throb of her heart . . . and his.

'Danton . . .' she whispered, for the sheer gratification of saying his name.

'Yes . . .' he breathed, and it was a sigh of deep satisfaction.

'Do you always make love . . . like this?' she asked dreamily.

'No.' He kissed her again, long and lingeringly as his fingers grazed around her breasts in tantalising patterns. 'Would you prefer some other way?' he murmured against her lips.

'No,' she whispered, revelling in the exquisite sensitivity he was arousing everywhere he touched. How could she resent him, or feel any aggressive hostility at all when he was treating her so gently . . . so lovingly?

'Did you feel . . . the same?' she asked.

'Of course,' he answered softly.

And she lay with him, content, not thinking of the past or the future . . . hoarding every moment as a treasure that could never be taken away from her, no matter what else ever happened.

CHAPTER ELEVEN

ANOTHER day . . . how many had there been? Bernadette turned her head to look at the man who was still asleep beside her, his naked body stretched out in graceful repose. He was beautiful . . . beautiful and sexy and infinitely dangerous! She didn't even know how many times she had let him make love to her.

The thought forced Bernadette to realise how deeply she had fallen under the spell of sensuality that Danton had woven. She had no control over what he was doing to her. She had lost all semblance of control the very first night on the beach—even the memory of that blissful coming together sent a squirming shiver of pleasure through her body, and she would never forget the magic of that night as long as she lived—but she couldn't keep on like this.

In an effort to re-establish some control on herself and the situation, Bernadette tried to count the days that had passed already, to remember each one in its entirety.

There was the day they had gone over the plantation and Danton had made love to her by the waterfall. And when she had complained that someone might come upon them, he had laughed and taken her under the waterfall and made love to her in the shallow cave behind it.

The other days were more difficult to separate: fishing; swimming in the lagoon; learning how to snorkel; and making love any time . . . any place . . . each marvellous experience blurring into another so it was impossible to recall a definite sequence . . . what morning or afternoon or evening or night.

Danton was insatiable. He lived as if there were no tomorrow, as if every day had to be filled with every pleasure there could possibly be between a man and a woman; and she had found it impossible to resist following his lead.

And that was the problem! He was turning her into a mindless, vapid, will-less person who responded only to his touch. She wasn't even waiting for his touch any more. She actually exulted in being provocative, using her body to excite him, deliberately inviting his kisses and caresses and . . . before she even realised what she was doing, her hand reached out and gently stroked down his outflung arm.

Danton stirred in his sleep, turned instinctively to press his body to hers, his arm lifting and curling around her waist before he sighed contentedly and was peaceful again. A glorious sense of satisfaction spread through Bernadette. She loved the feel of him next to her. She loved . . .

The revelation struck her with shattering force! Danton was making her fall in love with him . . . hopelessly, blindly, mindlessly in love!

Fear churned through Bernadette.

'To make you love me' . . . that was what Danton had said that first night on the beach! Nothing about loving her!

Her mind flashed through all Danton had said to her the day she had arrived on the island . . .

It would have been no great triumph for him to have seduced her six years ago when she had been young and innocent. He had waited for her to become a more worthy target . . . a spicier challenge . . .

And the judgement about the island . . . there was no gamble involved at all—if he made her love him! If he exacted that most total of surrenders from her, then she would give him anything—herself, the island, anything—just as she had been doing! What sweeter victory could he have over the girl-woman who had scorned him and all he was?

The bitter irony of it clawed through her heart. All these years of never being loved, of never having anyone to love . . . she hadn't even comprehended the depth of the need that Danton had tapped . . . how could she, when she had lived all her life without love? She hadn't known, hadn't guessed . . . but Danton had, she suddenly realised . . . and that was the bitterest cut of all!

For Danton to make her love him was the cruellest and most tyrannical thing he could do to her . . . and that had been his terrible scheme all along. She could see through it now.

He stirred again, his hand sliding up to curl over

her breast. Even in his sleep Danton could keep her tied to him! And if he woke she would be almost instantly be plunged back into the thraldom of loving and feeling loved. Danton could drive her to the stage of passion where every neurone in her brain was screaming for release. And that was his power over her.

She had to stop it! Stop it now before she lost her will to survive without him! It was all very well for him to enjoy being a voluptuary. One woman meant no more than another. But she wasn't like that, could never be, and it would kill her when he sent her away at the end of the allotted time.

She had let herself get too soft . . . putty in his hands. And since she had no way off the island, nowhere to hide, no one else to call on for help . . . she had to find and stick to some kind of effective stand against what Danton was doing to her. Erect barriers that could hold strong and steady!

Trembling from the effort required to break free of him, Bernadette lifted his hand from her body and slid off the king-size bed. She padded silently through the bungalow, pausing only on the front porch to drag on the bottom half of her bikini which had been left to dry on a chair.

She couldn't even remember where the bra-top was. Danton had discarded it days ago. And it had felt great not to be bothered with clothes, to be free and natural and . . . and if she didn't pull herself up soon, she would find it impossible to fit back into any normal life.

Her gaze skated bleakly around the graceful

palm trees, the brilliant white stretch of beach, the inviting waters of the turquoise lagoon. This wasn't the real world. She had to keep remembering that! This fantasy of love in paradise would come to an end after thirty days, and then . . . she had trained to be a doctor. It was what she had wanted to be . . . what she would be . . .

And even that Danton had used to serve his purpose! He was seducing her mind as well as her body. It was so diabolically clever and ruthlessly thorough of Danton to have used the birth of Marita's baby to make her feel valued and needed . . . and loved!

He had played his part flawlessly, getting her there in time after Ariitea had sent Tanoa for the *taote's* help; and then calming the distressed girl while Bernadette worked on keeping the baby alive.

The breach birth had been difficult, the umbilical cord being pushed into the birth canal ahead of the baby so that the risk of the baby's blood supply being cut off during birth had been frightening.

The joy of delivering that baby safely . . . and the relief! It had been wonderful—worth all the years of study and training—and Danton had said quietly to her, 'You are needed here, Bernadette. And one day, when you are ready, we will have a baby too.'

She had felt so triumphant and happy, and even now she wanted to believe him. Maybe it wasn't all a cruel, heartless game! Maybe she had it wrong, and he wanted their relationship to go on and on, not ending when the thirty days were over. What if he did love her? Or did he mean having a baby like Marita . . . like her own mother . . . without benefit of marriage?

Her mind started going around in chaotic circles. Hope and need urged her for a stay of judgement . . . let everything go on as it was. Wait and see. But the fear of losing, of ceding all control to Danton, only to be cast aside. How could she bear it if that happened?

Desperate for some relief from her tortured thoughts, Bernadette picked up the book she had been reading from time to time. It was a collection of stories which were set in the Polynesian islands, and she had enjoyed each one she had read so far. More than enjoyed them. The man who had written them knew about life. And love!

She glanced down at the author's name—Jacques Henri—and wondered who he was, where he lived, and how he had come to have such a deep and sensitive understanding of people.

Of all the books she had read—all the authors—none had been so attuned to her own heart and mind as this one. Everything was so right to her. Not one false note or tone anywhere. Each story had given her immense satisfaction, both mentally and emotionally, and when she went home she would certainly look for more books by him. They might provide some solace.

Bernadette heaved a miserable sigh. Jacques Henri was the kind of man she should fall in love with, not a ruthless game-player like Danton Fayette.

She tried to quell the sense of helplessness that tore at her mind, but could find no real strength of purpose for anything. In a half-hearted bid to get away from the man who had gathered so much power over her, she carried the book out to the beach.

The pandanus mats which they used for sunbathing were coated with sand. She shook one of them, laid it straight again, then stretched out on it. The book fell open at her marker, but, no matter how deeply she admired the author's sensitive handling of his subject, Bernadette couldn't concentrate on the written word when her own emotions were so totally jumbled.

'Thinking of reading?'

Danton's lightly mocking voice sent a shiver of apprehension down her spine. How long had he been watching her, noting that she hadn't turned a page? Did he have any genuine feeling for her beyond the desire that might soon be sated? She glanced up and knew he was about to start on her again. And she had no defences ready. Particularly not when he hadn't bothered with any clothing at all.

'You should have woken me,' he chided, and dropped on to the mat beside her. His fingers feathered down the curve of her back and he pressed a soft, warm kiss on her shoulder.

Bernadette tried to think of what she should say . . . but already her skin was purring with pleasure.

'My grandfather used to tell me stories like those. I'm glad you like them,' Danton said lazily, and his fingers slid teasingly along the elastic edge of her bikini pants. 'Let's take this off.'

She gritted her teeth, determined to make a stand against giving in to Danton all the time. If she did not grasp back some control she was completely lost.

'No, Danton,' she said as firmly as she could. 'The time for understanding each other has come.'

'That's true,' he conceded happily, content to caress the smooth satin of her skin and play with the long silk of her hair.

It was terribly distracting. Bernadette couldn't think what to say next. Her whole being was so intensely focused on what he was doing that any idea of control simply floated away. 'Let's swim,' she said huskily, and ran down into the warm water of the lagoon.

But Danton caught her, as she knew he would, as she wanted him to. Some remnant of sanity kept telling Bernadette it was madness—a game with rules she didn't know and couldn't play to. But Danton knew. He could hold her against him and send her mindless with bliss. He was in control. *The most dangerous man alive!*

But she was alive too . . . fantastically alive to the wonderful warmth of the water, the bright sparkle of the morning sun, the brilliant blue of the sky; and Danton . . . Danton pressing into her, shattering all her feverish thoughts of making any kind of judgement.

Once again Bernadette succumbed to the magic he wove with all the art of a great enchanter. She was his creature, every vital pulse-beat of her existence bound to his—possessor and possessed. And all the deep, turbulent feelings he stirred cried out to be met and answered in kind.

But when it was finished, all Danton did was smile and say, 'Do you feel better now?'

Bernadette's heart squeezed into a painful knot. It hadn't meant any more to him than a physical release of tension! Lovers in a sexual sense . . . that was all he had ever meant. To even want to believe anything else was blindly foolish. And she knew that the pain she felt now could only get worse. She had only one recourse, and no matter that it wrenched her apart, she had to take it.

'Danton . . .' How hard it was to say! 'I don't want you to be offended, but . . .'

'Impossible to offend me,' he said laughingly.

She said it fast, before the words could choke in her throat. 'I want to leave the island!'

The laughter in his eyes wavered into mocking disbelief. 'Why?'

'You're bad for me, Danton,' she cried, trying to hang on to some mental sanity.

'Nonsense! I am good for you. You glow with happiness. In all the time you've been here, you haven't suffered one asthma attack. Your body sings with well-being. Can you tell me it's not so?' he demanded, and bent down to kiss her breasts. His arm scooped her legs out from under her and he floated her on the water, giving her no leverage at all to move away from him.

The sweet, piercing shafts of pleasure ripped through Bernadette's body, and she moaned as she struggled against the insidious power he held over her. It was only physical . . . physical . . . her mind screamed against the treachery of her response to him. She had to claw back some real control before it was too late. She didn't mean anything to him. He had wanted her and he was having his way with her. That was all. And he didn't care if she was destroyed when he finished with her.

'Stop it!' She tried to say the words firmly even as she writhed under his caresses, wanting him to go on.

He knew it. Of course he knew it. His eyes danced wicked darts of desire at her. She shut her own against him, against his ruthless manipulation, and painfully gathered the only defiance that denied him an absolute surrender from her.

'I will never love you, Danton.'

And the sweet torment stopped. She heard Danton draw in a deep breath, then he pulled her up into his arms, pressing the full persuasion of his body against hers. He kissed her eyelids, gently teasing them open.

'Stay the full time. It's only another twenty days. Let me change your mind,' he said softly. 'You will come to love me. I promise you that.'

He did not have to promise. If it wasn't true now, it was so close to being true it didn't matter. Bernadette wanted to believe that the dark turbulence in his eyes meant that he truly cared for her, but the twenty-day deadline was too much of a stumbling-block. She was nearly lost already. In another twenty days he would own her entirely.

That was the challenge he had set himself, and he hadn't lost track of the days. He had a timetable clicking away in his damnably calculating mind. And after he had drawn all he had wanted from her, after she had decided the fate of the island in his favour, he would then send her away. And she would have hurt her father as well as herself.

Her eyes accused him with what she knew. 'I want you to let me go, Danton. I'm only the pleasure of the moment to you.'

His face sharpened. His hands slid from her back to her arms, releasing her from his embrace but still holding her fast. 'That's not exactly right, Bernadette,' he said quietly. 'You are the pleasure of *all* my moments.'

The words tore at her brittle defences, and as if he sensed his advantage Danton's face relaxed into an expression of tenderness. He lifted his hands to stroke the hair away from her face. His eyes held a dark, hypnotic softness as he spoke, drawing on the vulnerability of her heart.

'Forget what you said. That was an aberration of the moment. Let me tell you the ways I love you . . .'

'No!' She dragged the word out in sheer desperation. She couldn't bear to hear his glib phrases of love! He had probably used them on a hundred women! A thousand, for all she knew!

She shook her head free of his touch and pushed away from him.

'It stops now, Danton. I can't go on with it any longer!' she cried vehemently. 'No more making love! No more anything between us. It has to stop. Immediately!'

She didn't dare wait for an answer or any other reaction from him. She plunged through the water to the beach and ran up to the bungalow, her heart hammering in fear that he was right behind her. And she couldn't let him catch her. Not again! She bolted into the bathroom and shot the lock home, then leaned weakly against the door, her whole body shaking in distress.

There were no pounding footsteps, no sound of pursuit at all. Limp with relief, Bernadette dragged herself under the shower and let the stinging spray wash the sand from her body. She couldn't find the energy to wash her hair. It was over, she kept reciting to herself. Finished! And it had to stay finished.

But Danton was waiting for her when she finally emerged from the bathroom. He rose from one of the cane armchairs in the sitting-room, his face grim, his whole body emanating a tension that reached out and curled around her. But at least he had knotted a pareu around his hips, so that the threat of his presence was not quite as nerve-racking as it might have been.

Bernadette was intensely grateful that she had left one of the native cloths in the bathroom the night before. However flimsy a piece of clothing it was, it did protect her a little from any move Danton might make on her.

But he didn't move. 'Why?' he demanded, his voice stinging with anger and the black eyes boring relentlessly at her mind and heart.

It was glaringly obvious that Danton had no intention of tamely submitting to her demands, and Bernadette didn't know how she was going to enforce the ultimatum she had thrown at him. But she had to somehow. It was the only way she would survive.

She reached deep into her soul for the strength that had carried her through all the lonely years of being Gerard Hamilton's illegitimate daughter, and forged it into immutable determination.

'Because I have a purpose in life. And this has gone too far,' she stated in cold, clipped tones. 'You're a very accomplished lover, Danton. I appreciate the time you've spent on me. But enough's enough. I want to go now.'

He shook his head, whether in reproach or disbelief Bernadette did not know. His mouth thinned into a savage line and a bitter mockery hardened his eyes. 'Can't you let yourself love anyone, Bernadette?'

'Certainly not you,' she retorted with all of her old fierce pride.

'Can there ever be . . . a right man for you?' he persisted.

The taunt scraped over the raw wound that he had cut into her heart, and the urge to inflict one on him was strengthened by her need to make her position impregnable. Unless she could nominate some man who had the qualities that would win her love, Danton would not let her go. And that would be the end of her. Inspiration emboldened her tongue.

'Yes! There is a man that I could love. Someone who would be right for me,' she asserted with proud confidence.

Danton's eyes glittered with some indefinable but dangerous emotion. 'Who?'

Bernadette lifted her head in scornful defiance. 'The author who wrote those stories I was reading this morning. He has the qualities I admire—a real caring for people, a deep sense of humanity. He has sensitivity, good humour, integrity—all the things that mean nothing to you, Danton. All the things that you are not!'

'How very enlightening! Jacques Henri could win your heart.' Danton's mouth twisted with savage irony. 'You could love a man such as that?'

'Yes.' Bernadette gave him a scathing look. 'A compatible mind has more lasting qualities than a compatible body. And that's why I don't want you any longer, Danton.'

'So . . .' The word hissed through his teeth. 'At last we come to the nub of the matter!'

His jaw clenched tightly. His lips pressed together in furious anger. The effort to relax was clearly visible. When he spoke his voice was destitute of any cadence whatsoever . . . a cold, flat recital.

'Let me tell you, Bernadette—and it gives me no

satisfaction—you have just made the greatest mistake in your life. And as God is my witness, I will never let you forget those words until the day you die. You are hoist with your own petard. Irrevocably.'

Bernadette managed a scornful laugh. It was the only thing left to do. But the cruelty in his eyes choked her laugh into a meaningless gurgle.

Her heart fluttered nervously at the dark, brooding passion that swept across his face. She saw the fingers of his hands clenching and unclenching. Had she gone too far? Was Danton about to lose control? She took a step backwards towards the bathroom, instinctively seeking protection from the black fury emanating from him.

His voice whipped across the room, stopping her in her tracks with its lash of contempt. 'Are you running from me . . . or yourself?'

Pride forced Bernadette to pull herself up and out-face him. 'I'm not running! I wouldn't run from any tyrannical brute like you!'

He stiffened at the insult. Yet strangely it triggered something else that climbed out of his barely leashed fury and superseded it. An aura of power surrounded him . . . the type of thing she had sensed in her father when he made a grand coup . . . the merciless stalk of the tiger about to stamp on its prey and go for the jugular. And that was precisely the feeling that pulsed from Danton Fayette right now!

'There is nowhere you can run to,' he drawled.

'Not even from yourself.' His eyes glittered with burning purpose. 'You see, Bernadette, however much you're going to hate me for this, you are going to face the reality of your own words. The truth is . . .'

'Mr Fayette! Mr Fayette!'

The urgent shout distracted them both. One of the islanders—Momo—leapt on to the porch and ran to the open front door, panting more words with a dark roll of his eyes. 'Mr Fayette . . . there is an urgent message . . . on the radio!'

'Go away!' Danton commanded, his eyes slicing back to Bernadette.

'Mr Fayette . . . it's too urgent!' Momo pleaded.

'Nothing is that urgent!' Danton insisted impatiently. 'Go away!'

'Message from a lady . . . Tammy Gardner. It's the *taote's* father. He's had a serious heart attack. They think he is dying. She must come quickly.'

Shock and horror drained the blood from Bernadette's face. She hadn't spoken to her father. She'd left it too late . . . too late! And there was no quick way off the island!

She turned on Danton, shrieking her despair. 'See what you've done! You and your ruthless, selfish games! My father was right about you. He had good reason to worry. And no doubt his worrying has caused this . . . this . . . he's dying, damn you! You have to get a plane for me straight away! I have to get to him. I have to . . .' She choked as tears surged into her eyes.

'Bernadette . . .'

Danton stepped towards her, seemingly in sympathetic concern, but Bernadette was having none of it. She screamed her torment at him. 'Don't you come near me! Don't even talk to me! You wanted to trap me here and have your own damned way! You've had your way, and I hate you for doing this to me. Hate you! Hate you! Hate——'

The sharp slap on her cheek shook her into silence. Danton's tight grasp on her arms held her still as he spoke quickly and curtly. 'I'll get you on the next available flight to Sydney from Papeete, Bernadette. I have a helicopter up at the plantation and I'll fly you to Faaa Airport in time to catch the plane. Now pull yourself together and get ready while I make the necessary arrangements. It will probably take an hour or two to get things organised, but you will get to your father as soon as it's possible.'

'You can get me off the island? Immediately?' she grasped dazedly.

'Yes. And if we can't get a commercial flight, I'll have my Lear jet flown out from Paris. But a bigger jet will be faster . . .'

'A helicopter . . . and a Lear jet . . .' The duplicity he had practised on her hardened her judgement of him. He had lied to her about there being no way off the island. All lies . . . to serve his purpose! 'You're rotten to the core, Danton!'

His eyes blazed anger at her, but his manner was controlled. 'There isn't time to argue about it! I have radio contact with anywhere in the world, so

I'll check on Gerard's condition before we leave. Now, if you think you can manage to organise yourself, get going.'

'I'll certainly do that!' she snapped.

He dropped a mocking kiss on her forehead. 'I'm so rotten,' he said, 'I'll send Tanoa to help you.'

Bernadette had to force herself to move away, to turn her back on Danton Fayette, and march into her bedroom. She was in a daze as she packed.

Less than two hours later they were in the air, swinging away from the island paradise of Te Enata . . . the beginning of the end of her association with Danton Fayette!

CHAPTER TWELVE

BERNADETTE welcomed the noise of the helicopter. She refused to wear the headphones Danton offered her. She didn't want to speak to Danton Fayette ever again, nor give him the opportunity of speaking to her. She wished it had been possible to leave without him. He belonged back there on Te Enata . . . behind her!

And ahead of her was the real world, her father, gravely ill but still alive . . .

Tears swam into her eyes and rolled down her cheeks.

There was no hope of ever reaching Danton. He didn't have any love in his heart. But her father . . . she had to reach him . . . they at least shared a kinship that could never be dissolved, and if she was ever to know any love at all . . . she had to get to him before he died!

They landed at the domestic terminal which catered for inter-island air traffic into and out of Papeete. One of Danton's associates met them and promptly transported them to the international terminal, speaking rapid-fire French which Bernadette could not follow. Danton left him to deal with the luggage and steered Bernadette away.

'The plane is already on the tarmac,' he

explained. 'Passengers were called some time ago. The luggage will be booked on the next flight out. There's not enough time left to get it on this one.'

Bernadette said nothing. She was intensely grateful that there would be no delay in taking a last farewell of Danton Fayette. It was disturbing enough having his hand on her elbow, walking beside him. The sooner she was out of his reach, and the further she was away from him, the better.

When they reached the departure gate there was no sign of any other passengers. A stewardess was waiting to take Bernadette's ticket which Danton handed to her. It was all over now. The end. The final separation. She would probably never see him again. But it was for the best, Bernadette thought desperately.

The ticket-collector said something in French. Bernadette automatically reached out her hand for the boarding-pass, but it had been given to Danton, who urged Bernadette forward . . . through the gateway . . . into the tunnel!

'Where are you going?' she gasped, every nerve screeching alarm. She planted her feet firmly on the floor and swung around to confront Danton. Her heart hammered a vehement protest against the suspicion that fevered her mind.

'You shouldn't be in here!' she cried. 'This will cause all kinds of trouble. Don't delay the plane, Danton. Please give me my ticket!'

'I'm coming with you,' he replied, his expression set with relentless purpose.

Her eyes flared with fierce resentment. 'No! No,

you're not, Danton! I don't want you with me. What do I have to say to make that clear to you?'

His face tightened, but the purpose in his eyes didn't even flicker. 'You might not want me at this particular moment, but this is not a time for you to be alone.'

'I've been alone all my life!'

'More's the pity!' he rasped. 'Whether you know it or not, you need me, Bernadette.'

'I . . . don't . . . need . . . you!' she bit out with scornful emphasis, desperate to escape his clutch on her heart once and for all. 'Get this through your head, Danton! You and I are finished! Thank you for the experience. As a lover I have to give you top marks. You certainly taught me things I can put to use in the future. With someone I really care about.'

The colour drained from his face at her contemptuous belittlement of all they had shared. Driven on by the triumph of having drawn blood, Bernadette delivered the mortal blow that would sever any hope of continuing their relationship.

'You are far too clever, Danton. But not clever enough! I don't like you. And I don't like what you represent.' Her lips trembled and she closed her eyes momentarily as she uttered the most terrible lie of her life. 'I could never love you, Danton. Not in any way. And if I had stayed the thirty days, you would not have retained the island. You would have had to sell it to my father.'

'You don't mean that, Bernadette,' he said bleakly.

For a moment she hesitated, but the pain he had given her was compounded by the pain he had given her father, and she gave the knife one final twist. 'That was my decision, Danton. So think yourself lucky that I'm going now. Be grateful for what I'm leaving you with. Be grateful for what you've got. For all the fun you've had, you didn't really have to pay too big a price.'

'Fun!' He spat the word as if it was anathema to him.

'Yes! And now you've got nothing more to offer me!' she said with all the violence of feeling it took to reject him again.

A cold, cold pride drew a mask over his feelings. 'You're a fool, Bernadette. Face up to the truth and change your mind before . . .'

'I was a fool to become involved with you. And I won't be a fool any more!' she retorted fiercely. 'And I don't want to see you again. Ever!'

A wash of anger and pain suffused his face, but pride stiffened his jawline. 'If that is what you want, so be it!'

He separated the airline tickets and slapped hers into her hand. The black eyes glittered venomously at her. 'One thing before you go. Something for you to remember me by . . . something you'll never forget!'

She already had that, Bernadette thought bleakly. She would never be able to forget Danton Fayette. But her decision was right. Heartache was all she would ever get from Danton. Heartache and despair.

His voice gathered a deep savagery . . . a sting of hatred. It whipped across the space between them in rapid bursts.

'What I was going to tell you before Momo came . . . what you need to know . . . what you must know! Jacques Henri—a man you could love—the man who could be right for you—that happens to be me, Bernadette! Jacques Henri is a pseudonym. My name—my full name—is Jacques . . . Henri . . . Danton . . . Fayette.'

She took in the bitter triumph in his eyes and her heart turned over. 'You . . .' Her mouth was dry. She felt as if everything inside her was withering, but she valiantly tried to hold back the terrible tide of desolation. 'You wrote those stories?'

Danton's mouth curled in contempt. 'You were my inspiration, Bernadette! From that day back in Hong Kong! It doesn't say much for your judgement, does it? I changed. You didn't! You had your *right man!* Unfortunately you didn't have the sense to see it. So go back to your father. I hope his illness is not as serious as they say. I hope he gets better.'

He gave her no time to take it all in, no time to revoke any of the terrible words she had spoken, no time to tell him it was all a defensive lie. He sketched a stern half-bow, and strode back down the tunnel.

The stewardess started towards them, hesitated as Danton brushed past her. He made no reply to her anxious enquiry, did not even glance her way. The stewardess shrugged and hurried on.

'Please . . . you must board now,' she said, touching Bernadette's arm to emphasise the necessity to move.

Bernadette reacted to the girl's urging in a daze. She was only aware of the dreadful emptiness that was creeping through her. She had forced away the man she loved . . . the only man she would probably ever love . . . the man who had loved her! She had killed . . . with ruthless, reckless ferocity . . . what she most wanted!

Impossible now to run after him, tell him what a dreadful mistake she had made. In these critical circumstances she had no option but to go to her father . . . her father who was dying . . . who might be dead before she could reach him.

The blackest of despairs clouded the first few hours of the flight home. Bernadette tried to tell herself that Danton had lied; he was not the man who had written those stories; he was too cruel and ruthless; he had played so many deceptions on her; she was right to have rejected him . . . but there was no conviction in her mind or heart.

She could not forget that first night on the beach when Danton had demonstrated a deep understanding of her needs—the kind of sensitivity that she had attributed to Jacques Henri. And all the days following, he had been good for her, caring about her pleasure and happiness, weaving a sense of togetherness that was all the sweeter because of the loneliness that had marked the rest of her life.

The terrible inevitability of the truth gradually

crushed down on her. It was she who had forced Danton to take the extreme measures he had employed to pursue a relationship with her. If she had not denied the attraction between them . . . if she had been more honest instead of shielding herself in prickly pride and fierce independence . . .

As she had done with her father!

Was that another dreadful mistake?

Had her father cued his manner to hers in these latter years, not daring to expose to her scorn a paternal love that had been so late in coming . . . not wanting to risk driving her further away from him by pushing too close?

Panic gripped Bernadette's heart. She had wasted the opportunities that had been open to her. She had closed the door on Danton. Even if she went crawling back to him now, he would spurn her as she had spurned him. She had delivered herself up to judgement . . . condemned by her own words and actions.

But her father . . . there could be no meeting half-way now, no fencing, no pulling back. She had to go all the way . . . if there was time. What did pride matter when there might be no tomorrow? She hoped he would be as honest with her as she intended to be with him . . . given the chance.

Jeffrey was at the airport to meet her. The old chauffeur greeted her with intense relief. 'Miss Bernadette, I have the car waiting.' He glanced around distractedly. 'Your luggage?'

'Coming on the next plane, Jeffrey. How is my

father?' she asked anxiously.

'Not good, Miss Bernadette. He's partially paralysed. The doctor says it's a miracle that he's still alive. I don't know what I'll do if . . .'

He bit his lips and Bernadette's heart squeezed tight at the sudden watering in the old man's eyes. She hadn't realised the depth of the chauffeur's devotion to her father, yet she should have. All the long years of loyal service . . . never a critical word! She had been blind to so many things that had been right under her nose if only she'd had wits enough to perceive them.

'Let's go straight to the hospital,' she decided. She understood that there had to be reasons why her father had neglected her for so long . . . reasons that Jeffrey perhaps knew. Or maybe only sensed. Whatever they were, whatever they had been was immaterial now. She had to live in the present, not the past.

The trip into the city was rapid in the Rolls. In less than fifteen minutes they were pulling in at the entrance to the private section of St Vincent's Hospital.

'Are Alex and Alicia here, Jeffrey?'

'No, Miss Bernadette. Only Miss Tammy,' he answered sadly. 'I hope you find your father well enough to talk.'

Bernadette found it difficult to speak over the sudden lump in her throat. 'So do I, Jeffrey. Thank you for everything,' she murmured.

Her father had been lonely . . . as lonely as herself all these years! The thought pounded through her heart as she entered the hospital. Neither Alex nor Alicia had been capable of any real communication with him, not on his level. And she . . . she had meted out niggling measures of her company! Tammy Gardner had probably understood him better than anyone. And Tammy had told her . . . 'he hurts over you'.

Not any more, Bernadette silently vowed.

She was shown up to the intensive care ward. Resolutions punctuated every step she took towards her father. She would bridge the gap between them, no matter what it took. And make him feel better. She had lost Danton. She couldn't lose her father, too.

His face looked drawn and grey in the white hospital bed! Fear clawed at Bernadette's heart. Don't let it be too late, she prayed.

Tammy Gardner rose from a chair at his bedside and came to her. 'Your father's condition is critical but stable,' she whispered. 'He's sleeping peacefully at the moment. It's the best thing for him.'

Bernadette breathed again. 'What is the prognosis?'

Tammy shuddered, then took a deep breath, but the pain in her eyes told Bernadette how desperate the situation was. 'If we can keep him alive for two days, Dr Norton thinks it's fifty-fifty. If he survives a week, he will live.'

'And the paralysis?'

'Would be temporary. In six to twelve months . . .' Her voice choked and tears welled into her eyes. 'I'm sorry. It's hard to . . . to see him like this. To know . . .' She shook her head, struggling to contain her distress.

Bernadette took her arm and drew her outside the room. 'Go and have a cup of coffee, Tammy,' she said in quiet sympathy. 'Take a walk. You need a break from the stress. I'll sit by my father. He won't be alone. And I promise you, if he wakes, I'll be the daughter you want me to be.'

Tammy searched Bernadette's eyes for sincerity and nodded her satisfaction. 'He . . . he should have died, Bernadette. Dr Norton doesn't know how Gerard survived the attack. The ECG was . . . was awful. I think he willed himself to hold on . . . for you.'

'I won't release him, Tammy,' Bernadette assured her. 'I want my father to live and I'll do all I can to make that happen. Go on now. He's safe with me. As safe as he can be.'

'Yes. Thank you, Bernadette.'

'Thank you. For loving him when I wouldn't.'

'I'll always love him,' Tammy whispered, and turned away as tears filled her eyes again.

Bernadette watched her walk away, understanding precisely what Tammy felt. She would always love Danton. So stupid and self-defeating to have denied it. She had the heartache and despair anyway.

She turned and entered her father's room, quietly taking the chair by the bedside that Tammy had vacated. It was hard to see him like this . . . so weak and helpless. And, despite all her medical training, Bernadette felt helpless too.

She listened to her father's shallow breathing, kept checking his pulse and monitoring the stylus that traced his heartbeat, looked at the drips feeding into his body. For the first time in her life she appreciated that, no matter how much knowledge you accumulated, there was always so much more that you didn't know . . . like how to keep her father alive.

She stroked his hand in the need to impart her own vital strength to him. How long it was before his eyelids lifted, she did not know. She didn't even see that first flicker of consciousness, but she heard the name that whispered from his lips.

'Odile . . .'

Her mother's name. Pain wrenched her heart. He had spoken it with such caressing love . . . and the look in his barely opened eyes . . . the yearning desire . . .

'Dad . . .' She didn't know what possessed her to call him that, but it tripped off her tongue in a rush of feeling. 'It's Bernadette . . .'

'Odile . . .' he whispered, but this time it was a breath of terrible loss, and he closed his eyes as his face twisted with anguish.

'Dad, please . . . you mustn't get excited . . . it's me, Bernadette.'

The ensuing silence was terrible. A tremor ran through his body. Somehow Bernadette contained an instant well of panic, and ran a professional eye over the monitors. Yet there was nothing she could do. At last another sound issued from his lips . . .

so faint it was barely audible. Bernadette quickly bent closer to his mouth to hear any word he might say.

'I couldn't help it, Bernadette,' he murmured, and she could hear his despair.

'I know . . . I know you couldn't. It's all right,' she assured him, not knowing what he meant but relieved that he knew her, and anxious to put him at peace with himself.

The words came haltingly, dragged out of a deep haunting regret. 'Your mother was . . . my love . . . my only love . . . so total . . . she was my life. We were to be married . . . we were to be so happy. I'm sorry I hated you, Bernadette. I was so wrong . . . so terribly wrong . . .'

She sucked in her breath at the shock . . . the pain of the revelation. But she had hated him too, and been wrong. 'You mustn't go on like this. It could kill you. You mustn't be upset,' she said with urgent intensity.

'Got to tell you why . . . so you understand . . . so you might forgive me.'

'It doesn't matter. Don't tire yourself,' Bernadette pleaded.

'So wrong . . .'

His head moved restlessly on the pillow, and Bernadette placed her hand soothingly on his forehead. His eyes opened and stared bleakly at her.

'You killed her, Bernadette. When you were born . . . you killed . . . your mother. And I couldn't forgive you. I blamed you . . . for the loss

I suffered. How can you ever forgive me?'

'I can forgive you anything if you loved my mother. I didn't think you did, and that was why I meant nothing to you,' she said slowly, hoping her words were coherent to him.

He sighed and his mouth twisted in sad irony. 'Even when I did come to you . . . I had to learn to love you, Bernadette. First, when your school reports were sent to me . . . you showed such strength. There was promise in you, and I wanted an heir that could follow me. It was cold-blooded . . . in the beginning. But I did come to love you . . . my daughter. To my eternal regret . . . it was too late.'

'I . . .' Tears brimmed her eyes but she managed to blurt out the truth. 'I love you too, Dad. I'm sorry I held back from you. I don't want you to die. I need you . . .'

His eyes suddenly sharpened. 'Danton?'

Bernadette shook her head. 'I closed myself off from him, just as I did with you. And I was wrong . . . terribly wrong. Don't let me lose both of you,' she begged. 'If you leave me, I'll be back to having no one again. And I can't bear it, Dad.'

He slowly lifted a hand and brushed the wet trickle on her cheek. 'So wilful and passionate,' he said softly. 'Not like me at all. Just like your mother. I should have seen it. But I preferred to see your likeness to me. Danton saw it all. I realised that afterwards. It wasn't a game with him, was it?'

'I don't know,' she sighed, and all the bleakness of her despair over Danton washed into her eyes. 'I don't believe it was. I think now . . . he really did mean to make me love him.'

'I thought so,' her father agreed on a tired breath, and for a long time nothing was said between them.

He appeared to sink into a deep sleep. Bernadette sat close to him, holding his hand to her cheek, regretting all the time they had lost, all that they could have shared together, knowing now that the kinship was closer and deeper than she had ever imagined it could be.

Tammy brought her a tray of coffee and sandwiches. Bernadette ate mechanically while she continued her vigil, willing her father to live. Hours passed. When he awoke again she thought he looked a little stronger.

'Bernadette, to understand Danton . . . you must see . . . only the deepest passion could create the patience to wait those years for you. To plan as he planned. To risk staying out of your life for so long. That was brave . . . I admire the man.'

But he hadn't stayed out of her life, Bernadette realised with a mind-jolting stab of perception! The flowers on her birthday . . . the mysterious love notes . . . making a subtle claim on her heart and mind that had made her find other men wanting in so many areas. Of course, it had to be Danton! And the sheer constancy of it . . .

'A passion like that doesn't end, Bernadette,' her father continued, and he gave her a sad little smile. 'I know. I remember with a keenness that never goes away.'

Bernadette stared at her father, wanting to believe it could be so with Danton, but remembering all too well that last flash of hatred in his eyes. 'You don't know what I said to him, Dad,' she said despondently. 'He'll never come after me again.'

A deep pride strengthened the lines of his face. 'You are my daughter, as well as Odile's. If you love him, Bernadette, stake your claim. And don't take no for an answer!'

Hope stirred. Of course her father was right. She hadn't fought to survive all these years to buckle under adversity now. Her jaw set in steady resolution. She would do the engineering for their next meeting. And no way would she let Danton get away with all the deceptions he had played on her! She wasn't the only one at fault. He had a lot to answer for. When next they faced each other . . . as God was her witness . . . she would be ready for him!

'Yes!' she said decisively. 'I'll do that.'

Her eyes flashed with the strength of purpose that Gerard was so familiar with, and he rested content. It was not what he had expected, not what he had planned for . . . life played such odd tricks. He had wanted to hand his empire over to Bernadette. But her happiness was more important than all the money in the world. Odile would have said that. Odile . . .

He closed his eyes, savouring the memory of the one all-absorbing passion in his life. Everything else paled beside it. All the wealth and power . . .

just vanity . . . scores in a game that didn't really count. Only Odile . . .

'Dad?' Bernadette, anxious for him.

'I'm fine. I'm feeling better now. Go back to Danton, Bernadette. Get it sorted out.'

'I can't leave you when you're so ill.'

'It's the best thing you can do for me. Send me a message.' He opened his eyes a glimmer and managed a weak smile. 'Tell me that you've won. Tell me I'm going to have some grandchildren.'

Her face relaxed into an answering smile. 'Only if you promise me you'll live . . . for a very long time.'

'Longer. I do not intend to miss out on the things I missed out with you. I want to be a grandfather to your children, Bernadette.'

Children . . . Bernadette recalled what Danton had said the night she had delivered Marita's baby. She should have known then that he loved her. Hadn't he told her that when he fathered children it would be with the woman he wanted above all others? And he had suggested that they have a baby . . . when she was ready.

She was losing her ability to think straight. Maybe that was what deep personal involvements did to you. Certainly when she thought of Danton she knew she didn't want to think straight anyway.

Bernadette rose to her feet and bent to kiss her father's cheek. 'You'll get your grandchildren, Dad.'

'Danton doesn't stand a chance,' he mused happily, and closed his eyes again, resting very content . . . having sent Bernadette on her way to the happiness she deserved.

Not only my grandchildren, but also Odile's, Gerard thought. And there would be no neglect this time. He had been taught the hardest lesson in the world. You couldn't blame children for fate, however bad it was!

Bernadette and Danton . . . Gerard felt a deep satisfaction. He would still get a worthy heir to his empire. No doubt about it. All he had to do was live long enough. Have that bypass operation. Another twenty years shouldn't be too hard to take.

And Tammy . . . he had to do something for her. Make her happy. And that shouldn't be too hard either. The older you got, the easier it seemed to be. She wasn't Odile, never could be. He had warned her . . . tried to dissuade her . . . but he had needed the love she had offered him, and taken it. Now it was time to give back . . .

He heard her tiptoe up to his bedside. He had always liked that perfume she wore. 'Tammy . . .'

'Yes, Gerard.' She sounded distraught.

He opened his eyes and looked fondly at her pretty young face. 'I figure on living for a good while yet. I know you said you didn't want marriage, but I'd like you to be my wife. Make it permanent. If you want to stay on with me.'

She drew in a deep breath. 'I love you, Gerard. You don't have to offer me marriage. If Bernadette said anything . . .'

'No. This is my idea. I think it's a good one. If you have to . . . think about it, Tammy.'

'If it's what you want . . . then it's what I want too,' she said with moving simplicity.

He didn't really deserve her, Gerard thought ruefully. But she would be safe with him. And he could look after her properly . . . give her as much pleasure as he could. As Danton would Bernadette.

The most dangerous man alive, he mused . . . but to have him on the same side . . . yes, that was no bad thing. It wasn't his doing . . . he really had nothing to do with it at all . . . but it was the grandest coup that could be accomplished!

CHAPTER THIRTEEN

THE island came into view, the cloud-wreathed peaks adding a misty enchantment to its compelling beauty. Bernadette prayed that Danton had returned to Te Enata after he'd left her at Papeete. It was too risky to enquire if he was still residing there, in case word got back to him. That would stack the cards in his favour and then he would surely deal her a merciless hand. She knew all too well how rejection could forge a barrier that was almost impossible to break. She needed surprise on her side!

The sea-plane skidded along the lagoon. A few canoes were launched from the beach, but her unannounced arrival was not greeted by the same festive numbers as last time. Bernadette glanced along the pier, but there was no sign of Danton. No jeep parked near the general store, either.

Bernadette opened the door of the plane as the lead canoe bumped alongside.

'*Taote!*' came the delighted greeting, and Bernadette felt a rush of relief as she recognised Momo. He could speak English. And she would get the information she needed.

'*Ia orana oe*, Momo,' she said, delighting him even further with her Polynesian greeting. 'Is Mr

Fayette here?'

'In his hut. He sent me to take care of business,' Momo said with a proud sense of importance. He gave her a huge grin. 'He will be very happy that you have come back, *taote*. He needs you to make him happy.'

Bernadette didn't think it would be quite so simple as that, but she put on a confident smile for Momo. 'Will you paddle me down to the hut in your canoe?' she asked, not wanting the news of her arrival to reach Danton before she did.

Momo agreed. The idea seemed to please him immensely. Bernadette thanked the pilot, handed her case and small carry-bag to Momo, and climbed down into the canoe. She was no longer the least bit disturbed by such a primitive means of transportation. Besides, she knew what she wanted this time and had not bothered with fashionable dressing.

The carry-bag held her bikini and a change of clothes. That was all. She wore blue shorts and a pretty patterned T-shirt with a low scooped neckline. Her hair was clipped up into a casual ponytail and she hadn't bothered with make-up. She didn't need or want armour against Danton any more.

'Your father is better?' Momo asked as he sent the canoe skimming down the lagoon.

'Yes, much better now,' Bernadette replied.

She had stayed in Sydney long enough to see her father off the critical list. Dr Norton was pleased with his progress and cautiously confident that he would make a complete recovery. Of course, there was no certainty that he would not have a relapse in the future, but Bernadette had no doubt about her father's will to live.

Momo beached the canoe directly outside Danton's hut. Bernadette thanked him and could barely stop herself from running up to the veranda. No sooner had she dumped her bags on it than Tanoa came to the front door, apparently expecting Momo's return. Her face lit up in surprise. Bernadette put a finger to her lips and quickly cautioned the girl not to give her presence away.

'Where is Danton?' she whispered.

'In the writing-room,' Tanoa whispered back, her big dark eyes sparkling with pleasure.

'Show me,' Bernadette urged. In all the days she had been at Te Enata, Danton had never taken her inside his bungalow.

Tanoa silently led her down the hallway and indicated a door, barely stifling a giggle as Bernadette opened it and waved her away.

Danton was sitting in front of a computer-screen, his back towards her. He wasn't working on the keyboard. He was half reclining in a comfortable office-chair, his long, powerful legs propped carelessly on the desk-top. Papers were strewn around as if he had tossed them aside in frustration.

'Well, who was it?' he demanded in an irritable tone, not bothering to shift his position or even turn his head towards her.

Bernadette closed the door behind her and took a deep breath. Just the sight of him sent her pulse skittering to a faster tempo.

'Bernadette,' she said softly. 'It was only Bernadette.'

His legs whipped off the desk. The chair swivelled instantly to face her. Danton's expression of startled disbelief changed quickly to one of stiff reserve. He rose slowly to his feet. His eyes skated over her, gathering a hard, glinting mockery before he spoke.

'Not your usual style,' he drawled. 'What happened to bring you back?'

She gave him a slow, provocative smile. 'My father needs a get-well incentive.'

Danton's mouth thinned. Bernadette could feel his tension, sensed the uncertainty in him, but she was determined to drive him into a full confession of what he felt for her.

'So it's the island you're after.' His lips curled. 'And you called me ruthless!'

She raised a challenging eyebrow. 'You did want to know of what steel I'm made.'

'The inflexible kind,' he snapped, a flash of bitterness in his eyes. 'You hold no further interest for me, Bernadette. Go and do whatever you want.'

'I shall,' she said, and walked towards him. She had to obliterate the damage she had done with her defensive lies. A few easy words wouldn't do it. He had forced her into accepting him. Now she had to do the same and force him into accepting her. She could only think of one way to unmask the truth and have it acknowledged beyond question.

'The problem with your mouth, Danton,' she drawled as she closed the short distance between them, 'is that it keeps uttering meaningless words when it should be doing much more marvellous things.'

She lifted her hands to his smooth, bare chest, but he stopped her from touching him, his fingers closing around her wrists in a vice-like grip. His jaw was tight, his face grim, his eyes bare slits of dangerous glitter.

'Don't play with me, Bernadette. You'll rue it for the rest of your life.' His voice was savage, unforgiving.

'You count that as *your* prerogative, do you, Danton?' she retorted mockingly. 'To play on people's feelings . . . to serve your purpose?'

'Think what you like! But be warned . . . there'll be no holds barred this time. I won't pander to your needs any more.'

'What about your needs?' she asked softly, her eyes giving him an open invitation to anything he desired of her. 'Don't you want me to pander to them?'

She saw the struggle on his face, pride warring with a violent urge to take what she offered. His mouth twisted with self-hatred. A low animal growl issued from his throat. He pushed her hands behind her back and slammed her body into his with punishing force. A ruthless cruelty blazed from his eyes as he slowly and deliberately ground her hips against his, stirring a melting softness between her thighs with the hardening aggression of his arousal.

'What do you want of me? Why come back?'

'Tell me you love me,' she demanded.

The breath hissed from his lips. 'You want us to be lovers again?' he snarled down at her, a black rage contorting his face.

'Yes,' she answered boldly. He could hide his love behind hostility—hadn't she done that herself?—but he couldn't hide the desire that throbbed from his body. And, just as he had disarmed her with his lovemaking, couldn't she disarm him?

'If that's what you want, then I'll oblige you, Bernadette. But not as it was before. I'll teach you the difference between love and sex, so you can recognise the truth. When you find someone you really care about.'

He smothered any reply she might have made, his mouth devouring hers with an angry passion that was beyond appeasement.

Bernadette didn't care. All the torment he had given her whirled into a similar violence of feeling that fed greedily on his loss of control. There was no gentleness, no sensitivity, no quarter given or taken.

Danton tore off her clothes. He ripped away his pareu. He kissed her with a wild ravening hunger; across her lips, down her throat, finding her breasts, making her writhe in a torment of yearning and need. She cried out, but there was no mercy in him. She clawed her fingers down his back and it drove him to a further frenzy of excitement. He lashed her quivering softness with the violent need of his loins, pinned her to him as he dragged her down on the floor.

The tension he created in her screamed for release, and Bernadette thrust her body at his in wanton encouragement for the final act of mating. He drove so deep and hard that her whole being convulsed; impaled, seared, shot into a thousand fragmented pieces that showered her with rivulets of ecstasy.

He plunged again and again . . . a torrent of sensation that crashed through peak after peak . . . tempestuous rapids that slapped and swirled and jerked her through one last shattering climax into a pool of blissful peace . . . a peace that was wonderfully ensured by the possessive clutch of Danton's arms around her.

Their sweat-slicked bodies revelled in sensuous contact long after passion was spent . . . long after Danton could keep up any pretence that she meant nothing to him any more. A joyful tingle of elation spread through Bernadette and she leaned up and kissed his cheek.

'Tell me you love me, Danton. I know you do. But I want to hear it from your lips,' she whispered seductively.

His chest rose in a quick intake of breath and fell in a slow exhalation. His muscles tensed and then he rolled, forcing her on to her back and pinning her there while the black eyes probed hers. His face was an expressionless mask, revealing nothing of what he felt, but when he spoke his voice gravelled over emotion that had not been fully controlled.

'Why would you think such a thing? I was merely teaching you a lesson, Bernadette.'

She answered him with the only hard evidence she

had, using it as a plea for his confidence. 'On my last birthday I received a card which said, "The power and the passion of life is in loving. Embrace the power; savour the passion . . ." I've done that, Danton. Now it's your turn. It's the loving I want. To give and receive. If you sent me that card, you'll know the last line written on it.'

She felt the tension slowly drain from his body. His eyes softened into dark liquid pools that drowned her in deep emotion. 'So now you know,' he murmured, as if it was a relief to him, a relaxation of control that had been a burden too long. '"All else is vanity",' he recited. His mouth curved into a half-smile of whimsical irony. 'It was what you taught me that night in Hong Kong, Bernadette. From that first meeting . . . what you made me feel. What I hoped I could make you feel . . . when enough time had passed for you to understand.'

He lifted his hand to stroke her face with questing tenderness. 'Have I?' he asked. 'Are you ready to be loved now, Bernadette?'

'It's why I came back,' she said huskily. 'I do need you, Danton. So much so that it was too frightening to contemplate what I would do if you finished with me after the thirty days. That's what I thought you meant to do. I thought . . .'

His finger ran softly over her lips, silencing the pain of thoughts that no longer held true.

'Bernadette, I had no hope. I was desperate. You have been so cruelly hurt in your life. How was I going to make you see how I loved you? If I had walked up and told you so, you would have cynically rejected it out of hand. I was gambling that the thirty days might be enough to win your love. But you started with so many misconceptions that I had to break down . . .'

'I know,' she sighed. 'I thought you were like my father. But I was wrong about that too. Even so, there's one thing I have to ask of you, Danton, or I could never be completely content.'

'Ask!'

'It's not for me. It's for our children . . .'

His face was lit by a radiantly happy smile. 'You want them?'

'I can't . . .'

His smile dimmed.

'I can't do to my children what was done to me, Danton,' she rushed on, needing him to understand. 'My father told me he meant to marry my mother, but I guess it wasn't so easy to get a divorce in those days. And my mother died in giving birth to me, so they never did marry. I hated being illegitimate, Danton. And it . . . it hurt very badly . . .'

His face gentled into tenderness. 'Did you think I could not see the pain in you, Bernadette? You had to prove so much to yourself before you could become a whole person. I tried to help . . . to direct you into paths of thought that would show you other perspectives on things . . .'

'All the cards . . .'

'And the roses, because I wanted to give them to you, and you would never have accepted them if you'd known they were from me. I knew the hardest task in my life would be to force you to the point where you would be willing and happy to marry me.'

'You always meant to marry me?' she asked incredulously.

He laughed and carried her with him to lie with her cheek pressed over his heart. 'My darling, I chose you as my wife six years ago. And after all I've been through to get you, I'm not about to have a change of mind now.'

Bernadette smiled. Her own heart pulsed with happiness, and in the bliss of absolute confidence she couldn't resist teasing him. 'I don't know that I can trust you, Danton. You can be very sneaky at times . . .'

'Only so I can do good things for you.'

She hoisted herself up to threaten him properly. 'If you deviate one inch off the straight and narrow, Danton . . .'

He gave a mock shudder of fear, but the black eyes were dancing with happiness, completely spoiling the effect. 'Never!' he said, doing his best to pretend seriousness. 'I'm too afraid of what your father might do to me.'

Bernadette laughed. 'That's another thing. We have to send a message to my father. He wants to hear that I won you.'

Danton burst out laughing. 'Victory in defeat! How typical of Gerard!' The laughter faded into a sharp look of concern. 'How is he, Bernadette? Was it worry over you that brought on the attack?'

'No,' she assured him quickly. 'He had worked out that you didn't mean me any harm.'

'A very smart man, your father,' Danton said,

relaxing again. 'But he is extremely jealous of you, Bernadette. He wants you to follow him.'

'Not any more. He wants me to be happy.' She constructed a very provocative smile. 'And supply him with grandchildren.'

Danton grinned and rolled her back over on to the mat. 'In that enterprise . . .' he kissed her very thoroughly '. . . Gerard will have my full co-operation.'

'Marriage or nothing, Danton,' Bernadette threatened as he began making love to her again with the exquisite sensuality he knew so well.

'Mmm . . . can you resist me, my love?' he murmured, melting her mind with his caresses.

'You're a terribly arrogant man, Danton Fayette,' she sighed, surrendering without the slighest qualm about the future she would share with him.

'Ruthless,' he said shamelessly. 'You can hate me for it as long as you like, as long as you love me too. I've waited too long to waste any minute I have with you, my darling. Now and for the rest of our lives together.'

And Bernadette had no quarrel with that. The desolate loneliness of her childhood years, the pain of never truly belonging to a family, the endless fight to be strongly independent—they were gone as if they had never been. Danton gave her a new world, and it glowed with a brilliant incandescence that encompassed all the sweet promises of life.

Coming Next Month

#1279 FLAWLESS Sara Craven
As a gawky, plain teenager, Carly had suffered bitter disillusion at the hands of Saul Kingsland. And she had vowed to get her revenge. Now, as an acknowledged beauty and successful model, she was finally ready to destroy him.

#1280 GOODBYE FOREVER Sandra Field
Roslin was trying to escape from a life that had suddenly turned sour. Tyson had a past that made him scared to trust the future. A chance meeting brought them together, and their paths seemed fated to cross. They both deserved a little happiness. Could they find it together?

#1281 A HEART AS BIG AS TEXAS Emma Goldrick
Stedman Colson behaved like a perfect neighbor when he moved in next door to Alison Springer, too perfect perhaps. The local sheriff was very interested in her activities—and Stedman was, after all, a lawyer. But whose side was he on?

#1282 BEYOND COMPARE Penny Jordan
Holly was determined to make Howard Neston appreciate what he lost in jilting her for Rosamund, and Drew Hammond was the ideal man to help her—after all, Rosamund had jilted *him* for Howard. It was logical for Holly and Drew to pretend to be lovers to make the other couple jealous.

#1283 ISLAND TURMOIL Annabel Murray
Chryssanti's puppy love for her cousin Christos was part of the past. But recently married Christos didn't believe it—and neither did his brother Dimitri. And Chrys was beginning to find that Dimitri's distrust hurt her far more than she'd ever dreamed.

#1284 A BEWITCHING COMPULSION Susan Napier
Clare had enough trouble preventing her mother-in-law from exploiting her son Tim's talent as a violin prodigy. But to be under attack from maestro David Deverenko was too much—especially when he turned his interest to Clare herself.

#1285 THE SEAL WIFE Eleanor Rees
Cathy's domestic services agency had met its first failure in the obnoxious Adam Dale, but she was resigned to it. That was, until the famous author Nick Ballantyn persuaded her that his friend Adam and his teenage daughter really did need her at their remote Yorkshire farmhouse.

#1286 DANGEROUS OBSESSION Patricia Wilson
Since her foster brother Dan had so cruelly dashed her hopes of winning his love, Anna had done her best to eliminate her obsession with him. She had nearly succeeded—until he suddenly returned from the Bahamas and crashed back into the forefront of her life.

Available in June wherever paperback books are sold, or through Harlequin Reader Service:

In the U.S.
901 Fuhrmann Blvd.
P.O. Box 1397
Buffalo, N.Y. 14240-1397

In Canada
P.O. Box 603
Fort Erie, Ontario
L2A 5X3

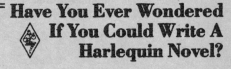

Have You Ever Wondered If You Could Write A Harlequin Novel?

Here's great news—Harlequin is offering a series of cassette tapes to help you do just that. Written by Harlequin editors, these tapes give practical advice on how to make your characters—and your story—come alive. There's a tape for each contemporary romance series Harlequin publishes.

Mail order only

All sales final

TO: ***Harlequin Reader Service***
Audiocassette Tape Offer
P.O. Box 1396
Buffalo, NY 14269-1396

I enclose a check/money order payable to HARLEQUIN READER SERVICE® for $9.70 ($8.95 plus 75¢ postage and handling) for EACH tape ordered for the total sum of $_____ *
Please send:

☐ Romance and Presents   ☐ Intrigue
☐ American Romance   ☐ Temptation
☐ Superromance   ☐ All five tapes ($38.80 total)

Signature_____
                                        (please print clearly)
Name:_____
Address:_____
State:_____ Zip:_____

*Iowa and New York residents add appropriate sales tax.

AUDIO-H

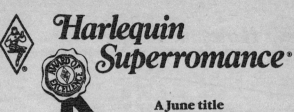

Harlequin Superromance®

A June title
not to be missed....

Superromance author Judith Duncan has created her
most powerfully emotional novel yet, a book about
love too strong to forget and hate too painful to
remember....

Risen from the ashes of her past like a phoenix,
Sydney Foster knew too well the price of wisdom,
especially that gained in the underbelly of the city.
She'd sworn she'd never go back, but in order to
embrace a future with the man she loved, she had to
return to the streets...and settle an old score.

Once in a long while, you read a book that affects you
so strongly, you're never the same again. Harlequin is
proud to present such a book, STREETS OF FIRE by
Judith Duncan (Superromance #407). Her book merits
Harlequin's AWARD OF EXCELLENCE for June 1990,
conferred each month to one specially selected title.

S407-1

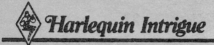

Harlequin Intrigue

Two exciting new stories each month.

Each title mixes a contemporary, sophisticated romance with the surprising twists and turns of a puzzler...romance with "something more."

Because romance can be quite an adventure.

Intrg-1

Romance, Suspense and Adventure